THE CURSE OF BACKWOODS

USHIKA SINHA

Made with ❤ on the Notion Press Platform
www.notionpress.com

Contents

Contents

Prologue

The moon hung in the blackish sky like a little silver fleck, its pale glow barely piercing the suffocating darkness that shrouded the alley. A cold wind slithered through the narrow passage, carrying the distant howl of a wolf and the faint scent of blood. The innocent man knelt on the damp cobblestones, his hands trembling as they reached toward the looming figure before him. His voice choked with terror, cracked as he pleaded.

"Please... I have done nothing! I swear it!" He breathed in and out, taking in rapid gasps. His broad, tear-dripping eyes reflected the flash of the blade before him.

He knelt before her, hands trembling, fingers clawing at the stoned floor as if he could dig his way to salvation. His breath came in frantic gasps, his eyes wide, desperate. "Please," he choked out, his voice barely more than a whisper. "I have a family... I have done nothing wrong..."

She stood above him, draped in red silk that clung to her form like liquid fire. Her lips curled into something between amusement and contempt, the dim light catching the rubies at her throat—glistening, crimson, like droplets of frozen blood. Slowly, she knelt before him, taking his chin between her gloved fingers. Her touch was soft, deceptively gentle, but her eyes were hollow, empty of mercy.

"You did nothing wrong," she echoed, her voice smooth as honey yet sharp as a dagger. "And yet, here you are."

The dagger in her other hand glinted in the low light, its silvered edge pristine—untainted, for now. It was a beautiful thing, crafted with care, its sharpness honed to perfection, meant to slice through flesh as easily as silk.

Slowly, deliberately, she pressed it against the trembling man's throat, feeling the frantic, erratic pulse beneath the cold steel.

A strangled sob broke free from his lips, his body quaking with terror. He shook his head violently, his wide, tear-filled eyes pleading with her—begging for mercy that would never come. He did not speak, too paralyzed to form words, but his silence screamed louder than any cry for help ever could.

She tilted her head, watching him with an almost fascinated expression, her lips curling into a slow, deliberate smile. There was no warmth in it, no kindness—only amusement, laced with something far more dangerous. Her gloved fingers traced the side of his face with an unsettling gentleness, as though he were nothing more than a fragile thing to be broken at her leisure.

"Hush now, dear heart," she murmured, her voice soft, yet dripping with cruel intent. "Don't fight it. It won't change anything. You see... sometimes, innocence is worth far less than opportunity."

And in that moment, as the blade pressed deeper, he realized—she had already made her choice.

CHAPTER ONE

THE SEALED GATES OF ELDORIA

The great iron gates groaned as they swung shut, the sound like the final note of a funeral dirge. The heavy chains rattled into place, secured by guards clad in darkened steel. With a final, decisive clang, the doors were sealed, locking the castle away from the world beyond. The city outside had grown strangely silent, the usual hum of life replaced by an air of unease. Something was happening. And the people knew better than to question a king's will.

Within the towering stone fortress of eldoria, King Aldric stood at the highest balcony, his sharp gaze fixed upon the distant horizon. From here, he could see the outer walls, the flickering torches of the city below, and beyond them—the vast, open road leading to his greatest uncertainty. His jaw tightened. His kingdom, once untouched by such desperate measures, now stood locked away like a prison. By his own command.

The halls of the castle had grown tense, servants whispering in hushed voices as they hurried through dimly lit corridors. Guards lined the main entrances, their hands resting uneasily on their hilts. The order to close every door, bar every entrance, had been given without explanation. No one in. No one out. Not until the king himself decreed it.

Aldric turned from the balcony and strode down the long corridor, his footsteps echoing against the cold stone. The tapestries that once told the stories of his ancestors now felt like relics of a time when peace had been an expectation, not a luxury. He could hear his own breath—controlled, measured—yet beneath it, a storm brewed within him.

As he reached the throne room, the massive doors swung open before him, revealing the grand chamber bathed in the dim glow of candlelight. The scent of burning wax and aged parchment lingered in the air. The vast, empty space felt suffocating, the silence pressing against him like unseen hands.

A lone figure approached—a messenger clothed in royal colors, his head bowed low.

"My lord," the man said hesitantly, his voice barely above a whisper, as if afraid to disturb the thick air of tension. "The preparations have been completed. The doors are sealed. None shall enter or leave until you give the word."

Aldric nodded, though his expression remained unreadable. He dismissed the messenger with a wave of his hand, his mind already lost in thought. He had chosen to close his gates, to shield his kingdom behind walls of stone and steel—but would that be enough?

King Aldric stood at the far end of the great hall, his posture rigid, his hands clasped behind his back. The heavy oak doors trembled as the guards pulled them open, and the cold night air slithered into the room like an unwelcome guest. Footsteps. Measured, deliberate, unhurried.

The other king stepped forward.

King Edric of Valesmoor, the soul's realm.

The man cut a striking figure—tall, broad-shouldered, draped in a cloak of midnight black, its silver embroidery shimmering like a sky full of stars. His face was a mask of calm authority, but his eyes... those cold, piercing eyes held an unspoken challenge. This was no mere visit. This was a test.

Behind him, his escorts entered, their movements precise, their armor gleaming despite the dim candlelight. Handpicked men. Loyal. Deadly. Not a single one of them looked at Aldric's guards—a sign of either supreme confidence or utter disrespect.

Aldric inhaled slowly, keeping his expression unreadable as he stepped forward to meet his guest.

"King Edric," he said, his voice even, controlled. "You arrive at last."

Edric's lips curved—just barely. Not quite a smirk, but enough to make it clear that he knew this meeting was one Aldric did not want.

"The roads were long, the night colder than expected," Edric replied smoothly, his voice deep, almost amused. "But I suspect you already knew that." His gaze flickered around the room, taking in the high ceilings, the banners of eldoria hanging proudly, the ever-watchful guards standing by the pillars. "Your hospitality is... thorough."

Aldric did not rise to the bait.

"A king must ensure his halls remain secure," he said simply.

Edric chuckled, low and knowing. "Of course." He took another step forward, closing the distance between them just enough to force Aldric to hold his ground. "Shall we dispense with the pleasantries, then? Or do you still intend to pretend that this meeting is anything but a game of blades hidden beneath silk?"

The room felt colder. The guards stiffened. Even the candle flames seemed to shrink. Aldric held Edric's gaze, his jaw tightening ever so slightly.

The air in the great hall felt colder, weighed down by something unseen. His fingers flexed slightly at his sides before he turned, motioning toward the long wooden table at the center of the chamber—a silent command.

Edric smiled, slow and knowing, before following. He moved with the ease of a man who had walked into the dens of enemies before and left unscathed. His cloak trailed behind him, whispering against the stone floor like the sound of a blade sliding from its sheath.

They sat. A goblet of dark wine was placed before each of them, the liquid deep as spilled blood. Aldric did not drink.

Edric, however, lifted his goblet, swirling the wine lazily before taking a deliberate sip. He exhaled in mock satisfaction, then set it down with a quiet clink. His fingers tapped against the wood.

"You rule well, Aldric," he said at last, his tone almost conversational. "But ruling is not surviving. And survival is never clean."

Aldric's gaze remained fixed on him. "Get to the point."

Edric smirked. "Very well. I come with a proposal. One that benefits both of our realms, provided you have the stomach for it."

Silence. The fire crackled softly in the hearth, the only sound in the vast chamber.

Edric leaned in slightly, his voice dropping lower. "Your kingdom thrives... for now. But even the strongest walls crumble under the weight of the hungry, the desperate, the useless. Dead weight." He gestured vaguely, as if swatting away the thought. "You waste food and resources on those who offer nothing in return. Criminals. The sick. The poor. And yet, here you are, locking your gates, clinging to an illusion of control while your enemies sharpen their blades just beyond your borders."

Aldric's expression darkened.

Because he had heard these words before.

Years ago, when another ruler sat on the throne—Queen Selene.

She had been ruthless. A monarch whose reign turned their once-prosperous kingdom into a nightmare of blood and sacrifice. It was under her rule that Edric had first made this very proposal, and she had accepted it eagerly, without hesitation. Children were torn from their homes, prisoners dragged from their cells. The poor, the weak, the inconvenient—all vanished in the dead of night.

The people of Eldoria had suffered, forced to live in fear, never knowing whose turn it would be next. And when the weight of her sins became too great, when the whispers of rebellion turned to screams of war, Edric had ended it. He had taken the throne, crushed her rule.

Aldric's fingers curled into a fist on the table. "Say it plainly, Edric."

Edric's smile sharpened. "A trade, Aldric. Bodies for power. Blood for gold. You send me the unwanted—criminals, beggars, the dying—and in return,

I give you what no kingdom can thrive without: wealth, soldiers, and silence."

Edric leaned back, watching him carefully. "Think about it, dear king. A kingdom is only as strong as those who serve it. Why waste resources on the weak, when their deaths could secure the strong?"

Aldric exhaled, his gaze locked onto Edric's. The room felt smaller, the firelight casting long, shifting shadows.

Last time, his kingdom had been ruled by a monster. And now, he had to decide—would he become one too?

CHAPTER TWO

THE CAGE OF GOLD

The cold stone floor sent a chill through Princess Evelyne's skin as she hugged her knees to her chest, staring at the grand chamber that had never felt like home. The golden chandelier above flickered with candlelight, casting shifting shadows across the marble walls adorned with paintings of long-dead royals—faces that had once been like hers, trapped in the suffocating elegance of their birthright.

She pressed her forehead against her arms, her breath shallow. She couldn't live like this anymore.

Outside, beyond the heavy velvet curtains, the world stretched far and free—the forests, the rivers, the villages where people lived by their own choices, not by the chains of duty. She had seen glimpses of it during her rare, escorted outings—children laughing in the streets, merchants calling out with voices rough from years of bartering, common folk who had no crowns but had something she never would. Freedom.

Her father, King Aldric, believed he was protecting her. Keeping her safe behind the palace walls, shielding her from the dangers of the outside world. But in doing so, he had caged her. Every step watched, every word measured, every decision made for her. The life of a princess was one of privilege, of silk gowns and elaborate feasts—but what was the point of luxury when her soul felt starved?

She glanced at the window, her heart pounding. Could she do it? Could she truly leave?

She had thought about it for months. Planned in whispers to herself at night, tracing imaginary escape routes on the cold stone of her chamber walls. She had heard stories of runaways—some who vanished into the wilds, some who disguised themselves as commoners and lived unnoticed among them. But would she make it? Or would she be dragged back, another failed attempt at rebellion?

Her fingers clenched against the fabric of her dress.

I have to try.

A knock on the door made her flinch.

"Your Highness?" A voice—her maid. Loyal, kind, but another set of eyes watching her every move.

Evelyne swallowed the lump in her throat, rising to her feet as if nothing had happened, as if she weren't just moments away from throwing away everything she had ever known.

"Yes?" she answered, her voice steady.

The door creaked open just enough for Evelyne to see her maid, Lissa, standing there with a polite but expectant expression. The older woman bowed slightly before speaking.

"Your Highness, the King awaits you for dinner."

Evelyne hesitated, glancing toward the window once more. The sky beyond was painted in hues of twilight, the last breath of daylight slipping beneath the horizon. The palace gates would be bolted a few hours from now, and the night patrols would begin. If she wanted to escape, she had to do it soon.

"Princess?" Lissa's voice softened, sensing her hesitation. "Your father will not like to be kept waiting."

Evelyne forced a smile, smoothing the fabric of her gown as if she could press away the weight of her thoughts. "Of course," she murmured, stepping forward. The moment she crossed the threshold, she felt the walls close in around her again.

The walk to the dining hall felt longer than usual. Each corridor was lined with guards, their polished armor reflecting the dim torchlight. The portraits of kings and queens past loomed over her as if silently judging her thoughts of rebellion.

By the time she reached the grand dining hall, the heavy wooden doors were pulled open for her, revealing the long banquet table where her father already sat at the head. He was clad in deep crimson and black, the colors of their house, his crown gleaming in the glow of the chandeliers above. His expression was unreadable, but his sharp eyes flicked to her the moment she entered.

"You're late," he stated simply.

Evelyne lowered her head slightly in apology. "Forgive me, Father. I lost track of time."

King Aldric studied her for a moment before nodding toward the chair beside him. "Sit."

She did as she was told, her hands resting stiffly in her lap. The table was adorned with roasted meats, fresh bread, and goblets of fine wine—food that could feed a village, yet it all tasted like ash in her mouth.

As the servants moved about, pouring drinks and setting the last of the dishes, her father finally spoke again.

"You've been quiet lately," he remarked, his deep voice breaking the silence. "Is something troubling you?"

Evelyne hesitated, the urge to tell him the truth battling against the years of practiced obedience. Would he even listen? Would he understand that his love felt like a prison, that she wasn't meant to rule, to be caged in a palace of cold stone and golden lies?

She forced a small smile. "No, Father. I'm just... tired."

Aldric studied her for a long moment before nodding. "You are to be Queen one day, Evelyne. There is no time for weakness." His tone was not cruel, but firm. Unyielding.

She swallowed. Queen. The very word felt like chains wrapping tighter around her throat.

Her fingers tightened beneath the table. No. I won't stay here long enough for that to happen.

Evelyne stepped into her chambers, the heavy door closing behind her with a dull thud. The flickering candlelight cast long shadows across the walls, but all she could focus on was the window—the only passage between her and the life she had always dreamed of.

Her hands trembled as she reached for the latch, feeling the cool metal beneath her fingertips. This is it. Her last chance. If she didn't leave tonight, she never would.

She turned away from the window for a moment, scanning the room with new urgency. What would she need? She couldn't take much—anything too heavy would slow her down. She grabbed a dark cloak from her wardrobe, something that would help her blend into the night. She had hidden some coins away over the past few months, taken from forgotten purses and the pockets of unsuspecting nobles. It wasn't much, but enough to get her out of the city, to buy food, to survive—at least for a little while.

Her heart pounded as she pulled on a pair of sturdy boots, ones meant for riding, not for the delicate steps of a princess. Every movement felt surreal, like she was living someone else's story.

A deep breath.

You have to be smart. Careful.

The guards would patrol the halls soon. The castle was designed to keep people out—but worse, to keep people in. She knew that better than anyone. There were only a few ways to escape unnoticed, and she had spent years mapping them in her mind.

The servants' passage.

It was narrow, hidden behind the great stone walls of the castle, used by the maids and attendants to move unseen. If she could reach it, she could slip out into the lower corridors, past the kitchens, and into the outer courtyard. From there, it was a short distance to the stables. She could take a horse, ride through the back gate before the guards changed shifts.

It had to work.

She adjusted the cloak around her shoulders. Her fingers trembled slightly as she extinguished the candlelight, plunging the room into near darkness. One last breath. One last look around.

Then, she moved.

This was her only chance. And she would not waste it.

CHAPTER THREE

THE SHADOWS OF THE MORNING

The morning air was crisp, tinged with the scent of damp stone and the faint aroma of roasted nuts from the kitchens below. King Aldric pulled his heavy cloak tighter around his shoulders as he strode through the dimly lit corridors of the castle. His boots echoed against the stone, a rhythmic, steady beat, but there was a storm brewing inside him.

He had slept uneasily, though the feast last night had been a grand affair. The wine had flowed freely, the court had been in high spirits, and Evelyn had been—

He frowned. She had been distant.

A thought that had come to nothing in the whirlwind of cheer came into sharp contrast with the silence of the morning. She had smiled, had spoken when addressed, but something in her eyes had been amiss. A glimmer of hesitation, a shadow of reluctance.

Aldric's jaw clenched as he approached the heavy oak doors of Evelyn's chamber. Two guards stood at attention, their expressions unreadable. He halted before them.

"Has the princess risen?" he asked, though the weight in his stomach told him he would not like the answer.

The two men exchanged a glance before one spoke. "Sir, she is not inside."

Aldric's fingers curled into fists. "What do you mean, 'not inside'?"

"We knocked at dawn, as per usual. There was no response. Upon entering, we found her chamber empty."

A cold dread slithered through his veins. "And the window?"

"Closed, Your Majesty. There was no sign of struggle, no note, nothing to suggest she left in a hurry."

Aldric's mind raced. Evelyn was not just any noble—she was his daughter, his heir. She was wilful in ways that both frustrated and made him proud. But she would not have left without reason. Had she fled? Or had something more menacing taken her?

He pushed past the guards and entered the room. The air was still, the bed untouched since the previous night. The fireplace had gone cold, and the faintest scent of lavender clung to the silk drapes. His eyes roved over every detail—the vanity where her hairbrush sat undisturbed, the books neatly stacked by the bed side.

Aldric exhaled sharply through his nose. He had fought wars, he'd been given blades in his throat, but the uncertainty of the future struck him in an awful way no battlefield had.

Turning on his heel, he stalked out of the chamber. "Call the captain of the guard. Now."

The command sent the nearest soldier scurrying, leaving Aldric alone in the corridor. His thoughts churned. If she'd had left on her own, where would she have gone? No—he could not allow himself to believe she had run. If someone had taken her, there would be hell to pay.

Minutes later, Captain Rodric arrived, his armor polished but his expression grim. "Your Majesty."

"Lock down the castle. No one leaves until Evelyn is found. Double the patrols at the gates, search the grounds, the stables, the servant quarters—everywhere."

Rodric nodded. "Do you suspect deception, Sir?"

"I suspect many things." Aldric's voice was low, dangerous. "Find her."

The captain gave a respectful bow before heading off, shouting commands to his men. Meanwhile, Aldric stood there, frozen in place. His fists unclenched and clenched again.

Evelyn, where are you?

The castle swelled with tension as the search began. Footsteps pounded through the stone halls as guards scoured every corridor, every hidden passage, every chamber. Servants were pulled aside, questioned about the last time they had seen the princess. None had an answer that satisfied Aldric.

The great hall, once filled with revelry, now stood creepingly silent. Aldric walked back and forth in front of the throne, each step deliberate and steady, but beneath the surface, his anger was boiling. He had spent decades in power, never allowing himself to give in to fear. He would find her.

A flurry of movement at the entrance caught his eye. A scout rushed forward, breathless. "Your Majesty, the stables have been searched. None of the horses is missing."

Aldric's frown deepened. "And the castle walls?"

"Guards are stationed at every post. No sign of forced entry or exit."

Damn it. She was still here, somewhere. But where?

Another soldier entered, this one older, his beard streaked with gray. "We've checked the servant quarters, the armory, the chapel. Nothing. It is as if she vanished into thin air."

Aldric's grip tightened on the hilt of his sword. "People do not vanish. Expand the search."

The hours dragged on. The sun climbed higher, casting sharp beams through stained glass windows, illuminating the dust stirred by hurried movement. One by one, the places Evelyn could have hidden were checked, yet still, no trace of her.

Then, a new report came. "Your Majesty, the eastern tower—her maid found something."

Aldric's heart pounded as he strode toward the tower, his mind a whirlwind of possibilities. He took the steps two at a time, his breath measured but his thoughts racing.

Inside the small chamber at the top of the tower, a lady-in-waiting stood, pale and wide-eyed. In her trembling hands, she held a delicate silver hairpin—one Aldric recognized instantly. It had belonged to his late queen, passed down to Evelyn as a keepsake. He took it, turning it over in his fingers. The metal was cold.

"Where did you find this?" he demanded.

"By the window, Sir," the maid whispered. "It-it was lying on the stone."

Aldric strode to the window, his gaze sweeping the view beyond. The castle grounds stretched out below, the outer walls standing firm, the forest beyond dark and dense. Could she have climbed down? Impossible. Had someone taken her through this very opening?

His breath came slow and deep. He turned sharply to the captain of the guard. "This means she was here, recently. And yet, no signs of a struggle?"

Rodric shook his head. "None, Sir. If she was taken, it was done in complete silence."

The thought chilled Aldric to his core. A forced abduction would have left something behind—overturned furniture, torn fabric, blood. This... this was too clean.

A memory surfaced—Evelyn at the feast, her gaze flickering with hesitation. Had she known something? Had she planned this?

Aldric's hand tightened around the hairpin. If she had left of her own will, he would find her. If she had been taken, those responsible would suffer his wrath.

The king straightened, his resolve hardening. "Send word to the outposts. Make sure to question every guard who was on duty last night. No one rests until she is found."

He would not stop until she was back within these walls. No matter the cost.

CHAPTER FOUR

THE EDGE OF FREEDOM

Evelyn's heart raced as she leaned in close, pressing her ear against the wooden panel of the secret exit in her chamber. The castle was still quiet, not fully awake yet, and this was her one shot to make it out. The servant's passage was her best route—quiet, unseen. If she could reach the outer courtyard, she could take a horse and ride far beyond the kingdom's borders.

She opened the door and stepped into the narrow, dimly lit corridor. The stone was cool beneath her fingertips as she crept forward, her breath shallow. Every step felt like an eternity, but she had rehearsed this route in her mind over and over. She knew where she needed to go.

Reaching the end of the passage, she peered out cautiously. The servant's hall was empty. She moved swiftly, making her way toward the outer courtyard where the stables stood. If she could reach a horse, she could be gone before anyone noticed.

But as she rounded the final corner, her heart sank.

Guards. More than usual. Their postures were tense, their eyes sharp even in the dim torchlight. Something had changed—they were on high alert. Had someone already grown suspicious?

Evelyn slipped back into the shadows, her heart racing. The main path was off the table now. She had to find a different escape route.

Her mind raced. The eastern tower. It overlooked the outer walls, and beyond it, the dense forest that stretched for miles.If she could make it there, she could climb down and vanish into the woods before anyone could stop her.

She quickly yet cautiously made her way back, climbing the twisting staircase that took her to the highest room in the tower. The air was cooler here, the silence almost suffocating. Her fingers trembled as she fastened the rope she had taken from her chambers to the heavy wooden beam near the window.

She tested its weight. It would hold.

Taking a deep breath, Evelyn stepped up onto the windowsill. The ground seemed to stretch out endlessly below her, but she knew she had to go through with it.

She held onto the rope with a firm grip and started her descent.

The rope chafed against her palms, but she pushed through the discomfort. With each passing moment inside the castle walls, her chances of getting caught grew. She hurried down, her feet scrambling for grip on the slick stone. The night air nipped at her skin, yet the rush of adrenaline propelled her forward.

Halfway down, her foot slipped. She gasped, gripping the rope tighter as her body swung away from the wall. The movement sent a jolt of panic through her, but she forced herself to focus. She was almost there.

With one last leap, she touched down softly on the grass beneath her. The eastern gardens unfolded in front of her, guiding her toward the thick treeline of the forest beyond. Freedom was just a heartbeat away.

She darted forward, keeping low, her breath coming in sharp, measured bursts. The castle loomed behind her, its towers stretching into the night sky, but she did not look back. She had to keep moving.

The forest enveloped her completely, its canopy blocking out the moonlight. As she moved deeper into the woods, the darkness seemed to close in around her, thick and suffocating. Towering trees twisted their gnarled branches above, creating a tangled ceiling that let not even the faintest hint of starlight break through. The air felt damp and heavy, filled with the earthy scent of moss, and an unsettling silence lingered between the trunks, interrupted only by the occasional rustle of hidden creatures.

Evelyn's breath came shallow. The further she walked, the more the forest seemed to close around her, like a living entity intent on swallowing her whole. Shadows shifted in the corners of her vision, twisting into strange shapes before melting back into the darkness. Every step she took felt a bit wobbly, the ground beneath her boots uneven and scattered with roots that twisted like snakes, ready to trip her up.

A distant sound—a whispering breeze or something else?—sent a shiver down her spine. She had always heard stories of the forest beyond the castle walls, tales of travelers losing their way, of spirits that lurked between the trees, guiding—or misleading—those who dared to enter.

From a young age, she had always heard the warnings about the forest. "Never set foot in that forest," they would say, their voices filled with fear. "Dark creatures and restless spirits hide among the trees. Those who venture in are never seen again, their fates lost to the unknown." This was the only narrative she had ever known—whispers from the servants, cautionary tales from her elders, and even the anxious murmurs of strangers passing through the kingdom. The mystery of the woods hung over her like a heavy blanket, making it seem far more frightening than any prison she could imagine.

Yet, she couldn't bring herself to stop. No matter how far the shadows loomed or how thick the night grew, she had to keep pushing forward. Her freedom was waiting just beyond this darkness, and there was no way she would turn back.

As she moved ahead, the air grew colder, and an eerie silence enveloped the forest. Then, in the distance, she caught a faintest flicker of movement. A pair of glowing eyes, barely visible in the thick underbrush, were watching her. Her breath hitched. Was it an animal? Or something else?

Her fingers tightened around the folds of her cloak as she quickened her pace, refusing to let fear take hold. The stories had always warned of dangers lurking here, but she was determined not to become another lost soul swallowed by the unknown.

A sharp crack of a branch echoed through the stillness. Evelyn froze, heart pounding. Something was out there. And she wasn't sure if it was friend or foe.

Echoes of the Lost

The evening sun dipped low in the sky, casting a strange glow over the kingdom. What should have been a tranquil dusk felt anything but. The streets echoed with the steady clanking of armored boots, while torches flickered in the hands of royal guards as they searched every alley, every market stall, and every hidden passage for any trace of Evelyn.

King Aldric stood atop the castle's western balcony, his hands gripping the stone railing so tightly his knuckles turned white. His normally composed demeanor had shattered under the weight of his growing desperation. Beneath him, the palace courtyard bustled with knights mounting fresh horses, messengers rushing in and out with updates, and servants whispering anxiously amongst themselves.

"Still no sign of her?" His voice was low but carried an undeniable threat.

A tall man in dark armor—Commander Gareth—stepped forward, bowing his head slightly. "No, Your Majesty. We've searched the palace, the town, and even the outskirts. There's not a single trace."

Aldric exhaled sharply, his jaw tightening. "Expand the search. No road, no village is to be left unchecked. If anyone is caught aiding her, they will answer for it."

Gareth nodded and was about to pass on the command when the king's voice halted him in his tracks.

"She would not disappear into the night without reason," Aldric muttered.

"Someone helped her." His gaze turned sharp as he looked at his men.

"I want names. If there was a traitor within these walls, they would not live to see another sunrise."

As his words hung heavy in the air, weighing down the assembled guards and officials, the sun finally sank beneath the horizon, casting the land into shadow. Yet, there was still no sign of Evelyn.

The hunt was far from over.

The streets were aglow with torches as search parties combed through every nook and cranny of the kingdom, their voices ringing out into the night. Riders sped beyond the walls, their mission straightforward—bring back the princess, no matter what. Guards burst into taverns, inns, and homes, demanding to know what anyone had seen. A sense of dread settled over the people as whispers of the missing princess spread like wildfire.

Inside the castle, Aldric strode through the empty halls, his footsteps echoing in the silence. His gaze flickered to the grand portrait of Queen Lysandra, her serene eyes forever captured in paint. For a fleeting moment, his exhaustion turned The hunt was no longer just a search. It was a race against the darkness itself.to sorrow. If she were here, she would have known what to do. She had always been the calm to his storm, the voice of reason when fear clouded his judgment.

His mind drifted to the memories of her—how she would sit in the gardens with Evelyn, laughing as their daughter attempted to chase the butterflies. He could still hear her voice in his mind, gentle yet firm, as she reassured Evelyn after a scraped knee or a nightmare. It had always been Lysandra who comforted their child, who whispered soft lullabies into the night when he had been too burdened by his duties.

Aldric took a deep breath, remembering how Evelyn's tiny hands used to grip his while she begged for just one more bedtime story. No matter how tough he tried to be, he always gave in—just for her. He had vowed to keep her safe, just like he had promised Lysandra before she left this world.

And now, he had failed them both.

His fists clenched as he turned away. He could not afford to grieve—not now. His daughter was somewhere out there, and he would bring her back.

The hunt was no longer just a search. It was a race against the darkness itself.

Aldric turned quickly, making his way into the war room where his generals and advisors were eagerly waiting for his next commands. The grand table was covered with maps of the kingdom, each marked with the latest checkpoints. He surveyed the room with a keen, unwavering gaze.

"Double the patrols near the southern border," he ordered.

"Increase guards at every major road leading out of the kingdom." His voice grew colder. "She cannot have simply vanished. Someone knows something. If any commoners withhold information, they are to be questioned thoroughly."

One of the nobles hesitated. "Your Majesty, if she left willingly, she may not wish to return."

Silence fell over the room like a heavy fog. Aldric's gaze snapped toward the man, his expression like carved stone.

"She is my daughter. She will return," he said, voice dangerously low. "One way or another."

The room remained silent as the men exchanged wary glances. None dared question him further. The king was a man who had already lost too much, and he would not lose again.

The rhythmic thud of galloping hooves, the shouts of soldiers, and the distant howls of hounds filled the air across the kingdom. Meanwhile, the forests beyond the castle walls stood darkly, their shadows consuming every bit of light.

If Evelyn had ventured there, she was beyond the reach of his men.

CHAPTER SIX

THE SHADOWS CALL

The forest closed in around her, dense and unrelenting. Shadows reached out like desperate fingers as Evelyn carefully navigated through the twisted trees. The chilly air clung to her skin, and each crack of a twig under her boots made her heart race.

She had been running for what seemed like an endless period, her breath coming in quick gasps and her muscles screaming in protest. Still, she pushed herself to keep going, venturing further into the mysterious darkness. The haunting whispers of childhood fears played in her mind like a broken record.

"No one who enters the forest returns."

"Dark things lurk in the shadows."

She shook her head, forcing herself to focus. Superstition wouldn't help her now. She had made it this far. There was no turning back.

The trees loomed like quiet guardians, their gnarled branches stretching out toward her, their bark resembling the twisted fingers of long-forgotten spirits. Just a hint of the faintest dawn light managed to filter through the thick canopy overhead, leaving her in darkness, depending solely on her instincts to navigate her way forward.

Then, she tripped.

Her foot caught on something, a root or a rock—she couldn't tell. Before she could react, she pitched forward. The world spun.

Pain shot through her as she hit the ground, her hands scraping against the rough bark and sharp stones. A cry slipped from her lips as she tumbled down a small slope, rolling through the dense underbrush. The force of her fall pushed her further down, leaves and dirt sticking to her as she fought to regain control. Finally, she crashed to a halt against the base of a massive, ancient tree.

Silence.

For what felt like an eternity, she lay there, disoriented and struggling to catch her breath. Her fingers dug into the cool, damp earth as she fought to calm her racing heart. Every muscle in her body throbbed with pain, and her legs shook from the impact of the fall.

The silence wrapped around her like a heavy blanket, stretching on forever, filled with an unspoken presence. The darkness wasn't just empty anymore—it felt alive, as if the trees themselves were leaning closer, attuned to her delicate breaths. Shadows danced at the corners of her vision, shifting just out of reach. The feeling sent a chill racing down her spine, yet she remained still, caught in the grip of both fatigue and fear.

Then she heard it.

A voice.

Soft. Gentle. Too close.

"You are not alone."

Evelyn felt her breath catch in her throat. She stood still, her heart racing as a chill ran through her veins. The words weren't shouted or even whispered; they seemed to echo in her ears as if the person speaking was right there next to her.

She took a sharp breath and shot upright, her muscles coiling like a spring, ready to bolt. Her heart raced wildly against her ribs, and her breath came in quick gasps as she pushed herself to her feet, dirt sticking to her palms. She whirled around, her pulse pounding in her ears. The trees stood tall and silent around her, casting shadows in the stillness. There was no one there. Nothing at all. Just the deep, unrelenting darkness of the forest.

Had she imagined it?

A chill ran down her spine as she pushed herself to move quicker, her boots crunching on the brittle leaves beneath her feet. She knew she had to keep going, to put as much space as she could between herself and the castle.

Then the voice came again, closer.

"You cannot run forever."

Panic exploded in her chest. She turned sharply, her breath coming in ragged gasps as she sprinted through the darkness. She didn't care about the noise she made anymore, didn't care if something was following her—only that she had to escape.

Branches whipped against her face, tugging at her cloak. The ground was a tricky maze beneath her feet, with roots curling like the limbs of hidden creatures.

A rustling.

Slow. Measured.

Something was moving nearby.

Evelyn sucked in a sharp breath, her mind screaming at her to move, to hide, to do something—anything—but fear held her in place.

The whispers of her childhood came back in full force.

"No one knows what happens to those who enter this forest."

"Some say the trees themselves come alive, trapping the lost."

"Some say the spirits call to you, leading you deeper, until you can never find your way out."

A chill of fear crept in, wrapping around her like a heavy blanket. The atmosphere felt different, almost electric. The shadows nearby appeared to deepen, moving as if they were alive, keeping a watchful eye on her.

Then, ever so softly, the voice returned, but this time, it was different.

"Let me in." The words slithered through the air, wrapping around her like unseen tendrils.

A cold shiver ran down her spine, as if an eerie force was pushing against her very essence. Her body tensed up, feeling as if something invisible was reaching deep within her, exploring, and searching.

A whisper brushed against her ear, though no breath stirred the air. "You are mine now."

Evelyn's breath caught in her throat.

And then she ran.

Her legs felt like they were on fire as she pushed herself to keep going, jumping over roots and weaving around the branches that hung low. Every part of her body was shouting for her to stop, but she couldn't afford to—especially not now. The whispers surrounded her, unyielding, like invisible hands reaching into her thoughts. The ground beneath her was rough and unstable, but she hardly noticed the ache from her earlier tumble. Fear had numbed all her other senses.

She had lost track of time as she ran, and soon the trees started to thin out. The darkness opened up to reveal a strange, vast space, and there it was—a huge, frozen lake stretching out before her. The ice shimmered softly under the dim light that peeked through the branches, with some areas cracked and others perfectly smooth. A sudden gust of wind cut through her, sending a chill down her spine, and she paused at the edge, her breath quick and uneven.

Could she cross it?

Doubt clawed at her. If the ice were too thin, she would fall. But if she hesitated too long—

A whisper curled around her ear. "There is nowhere left to run, Evelyn."

Her heart raced wildly in her chest. She could feel the presence looming just behind her.

With no other choice, Evelyn took a deep breath and stepped onto the ice.

Every step she took sent a sharp crackling sound echoing across the vast emptiness. The cold seeped through her boots, chilling her to the bone as she carefully pressed on. Her breath came out in shaky bursts, each exhale creating a mist that hung in the air for a moment before disappearing into the icy atmosphere.

The ice creaked under her weight, but she kept moving forward, her gaze sweeping over the endless, frozen expanse. She couldn't bring herself to look back. The voice had fallen silent, yet she could still sense it there, hovering just out of reach, biding its time.

A few more steps. Just a little further.

Then, it happened.

A sharp, sickening crack split the silence. Evelyn's breath caught in her throat. She froze, her pulse roaring in her ears.

Another crack. And another.

The ice below her quivered slightly.

Her stomach lurched as she realized—
The ice had broken.

CHAPTER SEVEN

BETWEEN POWER AND PANIC

King Aldric leaned against the balcony railing of his war chamber, staring out at the ominous horizon. The torches flickered below, their flames dancing in the wind and throwing restless shadows on the castle walls. The night buzzed with tension—the quick footsteps of messengers, the distant sound of hooves as scouts made their way back, and the quiet whispers of his knights, all bringing the same unsettling news.

His daughter was still missing.

The knights had searched high and low throughout the kingdom. They sent messengers to every outpost, but still—nothing. That sinking feeling settled heavily in his chest. His daughter, his sole heir, was missing. And to make matters worse, the rumors had started to spread.

The nobles gathered not because they were worried, but because they had to. A missing princess was not just a father's nightmare—it was a political disaster.

Aldric's grip tightened. Was she taken? Had she run? Or had something worse befallen her?

The silence in the throne room was broken by Chancellor Eldrin, his voice smooth but edged with the careful calculation that had always defined him.

"Your Majesty, there's a sense of unease in the kingdom. Our search hasn't turned up anything, and the people are starting to murmur among themselves."

Aldric turned sharply, his gaze like a blade. "Whisper what, Chancellor?"

Eldrin hesitated for only a moment. "That she has been taken. Or worse, that she has fled."

A hush fell over the room. The weight of the words hung in the air, pressing down on Aldric like a boulder on his chest. He clenched his fists.

"She did not flee," he said, his voice hard as steel.

Across the hall, Lord Gregor of Blackmere—one of the oldest noble houses—spoke up, his voice a deep rumble. "If this were an abduction, then it is an act of war. If it was treason... then it is a sign of rot within the court itself."

Murmurs of agreement rippled through the hall.

Lady Selene, a shrewd and cunning member of the high council, narrowed her sharp blue eyes. "Your Majesty, if she was taken, we must identify the enemy swiftly. If she fled, we must understand why."

Aldric's gaze snapped to her. "You believe my daughter would abandon her kingdom?"

Selene tilted her head, ever the careful politician. "I believe the court must prepare for every possibility, Your Majesty."

Aldric exhaled sharply, reigning in his temper. "The search continues. She will be found."

Eldrin took a step closer and said, "I hope you'll forgive me, Your Majesty, but while the knights ride across the kingdom and search the villages, we in the nobility can't just sit back and do nothing. There are... other important issues that need our focus."

Aldric's patience thinned. "Speak plainly, Chancellor."

Eldrin folded his hands before him. "The question of succession, Your Majesty."

A cold silence fell over the room.

Aldric's fingers curled into fists. "My daughter is not dead."

Marlow lowered his head a bit. "Absolutely not, Your Majesty. But if the worst were to happen, the council needs to think about the future of the realm."

Aldric rose to his feet, his voice cold as steel. "I have tolerated this line of discussion long enough. Evelyn will return. Until then, any talk of succession is treasonous."

The court fell silent.

But Aldric could see it in their eyes—the doubt, the calculation. They did not fear for Evelyn. They feared for the crown.

And some, he suspected, saw this as an opportunity.

After the assembly dispersed, Aldric remained in the throne room, his thoughts heavy. The air smelled of burning tallow and cold stone, the banners of his ancestors hanging motionless in the dim candlelight.

He was not alone.

Lord Gregor, his most trusted general, stood at his side. "They smell weakness, Your Majesty. The moment they believe the throne is unguarded, they will strike."

Aldric exhaled, rubbing a hand over his temple. "I know."

Gregor hesitated, then spoke lowly. "Do you believe it was treason?"

"I do not know," Aldric admitted. "But if it was... I will burn every traitor to the ground."

Gregor nodded grimly. "Then we must prepare."

Aldric turned his gaze toward the towering windows of the chamber, beyond which the sky was darkening. His knights searched the kingdom. The court plotted in whispers. And somewhere, Evelyn was still out there.

He would find her.

No matter the cost.

CHAPTER EIGHT

BENEATH THE ICE

A deep, unending void enveloped Evelyn, dragging her down into its chilling grasp. The frigid water pressed against her lungs, stinging like fire while simultaneously numbing her limbs. She floated, weightless, as the edges of her awareness flickered like a fading flame.

And then—light.

It started as a faint flicker, almost imperceptible, but gradually it grew more intense, glowing like the cozy warmth of a fire on a chilly winter evening. It pierced through the darkness, unfurling in delicate ribbons that wrapped around her, easing the heavy burden on her chest. The biting cold faded away, giving way to a gentler, more familiar sensation.

She was no longer drowning.

She was home

Evelyn blinked, finding herself standing in the castle gardens, the scent of fresh roses and lavender filling the air. The warmth of the midday sun kissed her skin, and the distant hum of bees drifted through the lazy breeze.

A laugh echoed across the garden. A child's laughter—light and unburdened.

Evelyn turned, her breath catching in her throat.

There, among the wildflowers, was her younger self. A girl no older than seven, barefoot and carefree, her golden hair catching the sunlight as she twirled in circles. She chased after a butterfly, her giggles filling the air like music.

She watched as the child ran toward a tall, elegant figure. Queen Seraphina.

Her mother knelt, arms open wide, and the young Evelyn threw herself into her embrace. The queen's laughter was soft, warm, filled with a love so deep it made Evelyn's heart ache.

"You caught it!" Seraphina smiled, brushing a loose curl from the child's face.

"I did!" the little girl beamed, opening her tiny hands to reveal—nothing. The butterfly had long since fluttered away.

Seraphina chuckled, tapping her daughter's nose. "Perhaps not, but some things are meant to be admired, not held."

Evelyn felt the words settle deep within her, a lesson she had long forgotten.

The scene shifted.

Now, she was sitting beneath the old willow tree by the pond, the soft shade cooling the summer air. Her mother was beside her, humming a tune as she braided Evelyn's hair.

"Mother," the child Evelyn said, her small hands toying with the hem of her dress. "Will you always be here?"

Seraphina's fingers stilled for a moment before she smiled, pressing a kiss to the top of her daughter's head. "Always, my love. Even when you cannot see me, I will be here."

The focus moved once again.

Queen Seraphina stood at the center of the ballroom, her sapphire gown flowing like water as she twirled, her arms extended toward the small girl before her. Little Evelyn beamed, mimicking her mother's graceful movements, her tiny feet struggling to match the elegance of the queen's dance.

Evelyn's breath hitched. She remembered this.

A memory from years ago, untouched by time. It had been one of those rare moments when her mother was not burdened with matters of the court, when she was simply hers.

Seraphina spun once more, then stopped, kneeling before the little girl, cupping her daughter's flushed cheeks. "Again," she encouraged, her voice soft as silk.

Little Evelyn frowned. "But I keep stumbling."

Seraphina chuckled, tucking a loose curl behind her ear. "You only stumble because you think you will."

The child's brows furrowed, her tiny hands curling into fists. "But what if I fall?"

Her mother smiled, the kind of smile that carried the weight of wisdom and love. "Then you get back up."

Evelyn's heart twisted.

She had forgotten what it was like to hear her mother's voice, to feel her warmth.

The music faded.

The ballroom wavered at the edges, flickering like candlelight in the wind. The little girl blurred, her laughter distorting into an echo.

No...

The warmth was fading fast. Evelyn could feel it slipping through her fingers, the edges of the dream—no, the memory—starting to fray like an old tapestry coming apart stitch by stitch. The golden light grew dimmer, her mother's gentle laughter becoming faint and muffled, as if it were being whisked away from her ears. She reached out, desperate to keep it close, but the harder she tried to hold on, the quicker it fell apart.

The grand ballroom blurred, its marble floors splintering into shadows. The warmth of her mother's embrace faded into a cold nothingness. The music, once so sweet and familiar, slowed to a hollow whisper before vanishing altogether. Evelyn's younger self flickered, the light in her innocent eyes snuffed out in an instant, as though she had never existed at all.

No, please...

Darkness crept in, swallowing the last remnants of the dream. The golden light collapsed, shrinking into nothing, leaving her alone, adrift in the abyss. The moment her mother disappeared, Evelyn felt it physically, as if something had been ripped from inside her, leaving a hollow space where warmth had once been.

Is this what dying feels like?

She couldn't feel her fingers. Couldn't feel her toes. Even the frantic pounding of her heart had begun to slow, each beat weaker than the last. The pain was numbing now, no longer sharp and biting but distant, as though it belonged to someone else entirely.

It wasn't at all what she had imagined. She had always thought death would be violent, cruel—something that came with screams and blood, with fire and steel. But this... this was quiet. Soft, almost. Like slipping into sleep after an exhausting day, like being cradled by something unseen.

A strange peace settled over her. Maybe she should just let go.

No more running. No more fear. No more expectations weighing her down like an iron chain. The cold wasn't so bad now, wasn't so suffocating. If she surrendered, maybe she wouldn't have to feel anything at all.

Her vision started to fade at the edges, with darkness slowly creeping in from the corners. The last bits of light from the surface above felt like they were miles away now, just a thin, broken line that seemed like it was no longer meant for her.

Her body drifted, weightless in the water, her hair floating around like strands of golden silk. She could barely remember the feeling of solid ground beneath her feet. The world she had once known—the castle, the corridors filled with whispers of courtiers, the burdens of duty—felt unreal, as if it had always belonged to someone else.

Her lungs burned, but only faintly. Even the need to breathe was slipping away, becoming a distant thought rather than an urgent, desperate instinct. She had fought for so long, against expectations, against her own fears, against the shadows that lurked in the unknown. But now, there was nothing left to fight.

Would it be so terrible to surrender?

The darkness seemed to call out to her, inviting her to come closer, offering a sense of peace, a break from the relentless fight. Her eyelids grew heavy, and she allowed them to close gently.

CHAPTER NINE

A Stranger in the Snow

The wind howled through the valley, bringing with it the harsh chill of winter's fury as it rushed over the mountains. The air felt thin, almost stifling, as if the cold was intent on engulfing everything in its path. With each step Eris took, the snow crunched sharply beneath his feet, the noise echoing loudly in the stillness of the vast, frozen lake.

The village was quiet this morning, more so than usual. There were no songs in the air, no chatter of children playing, no firewood being chopped. It was as if the world itself had paused, holding its breath.

Eris frowned, his fingers digging into the rough stone of the elder's hut as he gazed out over the lake. The ice that lay before him should have been solid and unyielding. This winter was the coldest in decades, yet the ice remained steadfast, just like it always had. It was the foundation of the village's survival, the very reason they built their homes and livelihoods around that frozen expanse.

But this morning, something had changed.

The ice was cracked.

Not just cracked. Shattered

Shards of ice erupted in every direction, resembling veins coursing through the frozen ground, as if something had burst forth from below. Eris felt a knot tighten in her stomach at the sight. This was far from normal. Nothing in this village could explain this—nothing but superstition.

But superstition, too, was real.

"Eris, wait up!"

He turned at the sound of his name, spotting his little sister, Kira, trying her best to keep up with him. She was bundled up in a cozy woolen shawl, her breath creating little clouds in the chilly air as she dashed through the snow, leaving a flurry of white behind her.

"Why are you going out there?" she asked, out of breath but determined. Her wide brown eyes were full of concern. "It's dangerous."

"I have to check it, Kira." Eris' voice was steady, though there was a tinge of anxiety beneath the calm. "The ice—it's broken."

Her face paled at his words. "The ice... broken?"

He nodded. "I don't know how. But we have to see."

Kira stepped closer, her voice dropping to a whisper. "It's the curse, isn't it? The lake—the spirits—are angry."

Eris glanced at her, one that was supposed to soothe her but didn't quite hit the mark. Kira was spot on. The village had long murmured about the spirits lurking beneath the ice. They referred to it as the "Cursed Lake," a name born from tales of children who had ventured too near and vanished without a trace. There were stories of shadowy figures emerging from the mist and eerie voices echoing beneath the frozen surface.

He had never believed it, not truly. But now, as he stepped toward the lake's edge, feeling the weight of something heavier than the cold in the air, he wasn't so sure anymore.

The crack in the ice was massive, reaching from the middle of the lake to where the forest started. Eris knelt at the edge, intently examining the broken surface. He could hear the faint howls of the wind in the distance, but aside from that, it was eerily quiet. There was no movement, no chirping of birds or rustling of animals. The entire world felt hauntingly still.

"Eris, what if it's a trap?" Kira whispered. "What if the spirits are luring us in?"

He didn't answer. His eyes were fixed on the broken ice, trying to make sense of what had happened here. Something had disturbed the water. But what? A wild animal? A creature? Or... was it something more?

A shout from one of the other villagers suddenly broke the silence.

"Eris! Over here!"

He quickly turned his head at the sound of the voice and spotted Old Man Jorah making his way toward him, looking pale and unsteady. This elder had endured more winters than Eris could even begin to count, and his keen eyes had witnessed things that would leave most men in disbelief.

"Did you see the ice?" Jorah asked, his voice hoarse. "Did you see what's... what's there?"

Eris nodded, stepping back from the cracked ice to face the elder. "Yes. But I don't know how it happened."

Jorah looked over his shoulder, his weathered face wrinkled with concern. "It's not just the ice, boy. It's what's come from it."

Eris felt his heart stop at the old man's words. "What do you mean?"

Jorah gestured toward the center of the lake. Eris followed his gaze and felt his blood run cold.

At the center of the shattered ice, there was something—something dark and unmoving. A body.

The wind appeared to come to a complete standstill as Eris fixed his eyes on the figure. It was tiny, almost blending into the vast white stretch of ice, but there was no doubt about what it was.

A girl.

At first, he thought it might have been an animal, perhaps a fox or a doe that had ventured too close to the lake. But no, this was human.

A girl, lying motionless in the snow.

Eris's breath caught in his throat. His first instinct was to run, to get help. But as he watched the body, something held him in place. He couldn't look away.

He turned to Jorah. "Should we go to her?"

The elder didn't answer at once. He was staring intently at the body, his eyes narrowed, lips pressed into a thin line. "You don't know what you're asking. There's something... something not right about this."

"Not right? What do you mean?" Eris demanded.

"Who?" Eris asked, confused. His mind raced. The girl was a stranger. But the elder's face said something else.

Jorah's voice lowered to a whisper. "The one who was lost. The one who should never have come back."

Eris felt a lump in his throat as dread slithered up his spine. He had always heard the stories, but he'd never believed them. But now, as he stood there gazing at the girl in the snow, an unsettling feeling washed over him—something was off, something that didn't feel right.

"Go get the others," Jorah said. "We need to bring her to the village. She's not from here, but we need to keep her... safe."

Eris nodded, but he couldn't ignore the knot of unease twisting in his stomach. He took off running toward the village, yet as he sprinted, a nagging thought lingered in his mind: the ice underfoot wasn't the only thing that had fractured. Something deeper had shattered—something ancient and far more menacing.

CHAPTER TEN

CARVED BY FATE

Joren had just wrapped up stoking the forge when he suddenly heard the hurried sound of footsteps. He hardly had a moment to react before Eris rushed into the smithy, his face looking pale, marked by the smudges of soot from the morning's firewood gathering.

"You have to come—now!" he gasped.

Joren frowned, setting down his hammer. "What's going on? Why do you look like you just saw a ghost?"

Eris struggled to catch his breath. "A girl—by the frozen lake—she's not moving. She's—she's half-buried in the snow!"

Joren didn't hesitate. He quickly wiped his hands on his tunic and stepped out into the chilly air, calling out for his wife, Alis, as he moved. It seemed that others had picked up on the urgency in Eris's voice, because by the time they arrived at the village's edge, a small crowd had formed, whispering to one another.

Joren pushed through, feeling a tightness in his chest as he caught sight of what had stirred up all the fuss.

The girl lay crumpled in the snow, completely still. Her dark hair clung to her face, frozen solid, and her clothes—soaked to the bone—still looked pricey, even in their tattered condition. Her lips had taken on a bluish hue, and her fingers were curled as if she had been reaching for something just before she collapsed.

Old Mother Edda lingered close by, her fingers nervously twisting the fabric of her shawl. "I warned them that nothing good would come of this. There are bad omens, I swear."

Joren ignored her and crouched beside the girl. He pressed two fingers against the side of her throat.

A pulse. Weak, but steady.

"She's alive," he said, exhaling.

A collective murmur rippled through the villagers.

"Gods preserve us, how did she get all the way out here?"

"No tracks," someone muttered. "Nothing but her. It's like she just... appeared."

Joren looked down at the girl's clothing again. The fabric, though tattered, was finely made. She wasn't from any farm or village he knew of. And the fact that no one had seen her before only deepened the mystery.

Alis knelt beside him, already wrapping her shawl around the girl's shoulders. "We need to get her inside before she freezes."

Joren nodded and scooped the girl up into his arms. She felt surprisingly light, almost too light, her body going limp as her head rested against his shoulder. He could sense the eerie chill of her skin and hurried his steps.

"We'll take her to Siora," he said. "If anyone can bring her back, it's her."

The crowd parted as Joren carried the girl toward the healer's cottage, whispers trailing behind them.

Eris stayed close, his breath still uneven from running. "Do you think she fell through the ice?"

Joren glanced toward the lake, its surface eerily still. "If she did, she should be dead."

That truth settled over them like a cold shadow.

If she hadn't fallen... then how had she ended up here?

And why did it feel as if something unseen had carried her to their doorstep?

***

The healer, Siora, was already waiting by the door when they arrived. Word traveled fast in the village, and she had prepared a space by the fire.

"Lay her here," Siora instructed, her keen eyes scanning the girl as Joren set her down on the cot. Her touch was practiced as she unwrapped the damp clothing, replacing it with warm furs. She pressed her hand to the girl's forehead, frowning. "She's colder than ice itself."

Joren and Alis exchanged a glance.

Eris hovered nearby, unable to look away. "Is she going to make it?"

Siora didn't answer immediately. She fetched a small vial from her shelf, uncorking it with steady fingers. "She's lost, wherever she is." Her voice was thoughtful as she poured a thick liquid between the girl's lips. "But there is something... different about this one."

Joren frowned. "What do you mean?"

Siora pointed to the girl's hands, which peeked out from under the furs. They were adorned with delicate, intricate patterns—not quite scars, not bruises, but something altogether different. Symbols.

A sharp intake of breath came from Old Mother Edda, who had followed them inside. "Markings like that..." she whispered. "They don't belong to common folk."

Joren felt an unease coil in his gut. Who was this girl? And what had she brought with her?

The wind outside grew harsher, rattling the wooden shutters. A few villagers exchanged nervous glances, as if expecting something unseen to knock upon the door.

Siora continued her work, warming a cloth over the fire before pressing it to the girl's brow. "These symbols... they are not of this land."

Joren folded his arms. "Then where?"

The healer didn't answer at first. Instead, she studied the girl's face, as if searching for something unseen. Finally, she said, "Somewhere old. Older than even this village."

Eris shivered. "She doesn't look older than me."

Siora locked eyes with Joren. "But still, there's something timeless about her."

The room was wrapped in a thick silence. Outside, the night grew darker, with the village enveloped in a chill. In the soft flicker of the firelight, the mysterious girl lay motionless, breathing softly, yet trapped in a world that felt completely out of reach for everyone else.

LOST IN THE UNKNOWN

The first thing Evelyn felt was warmth—an unfamiliar, heavy warmth pressing down on her limbs. It was a stark contrast to the last thing she remembered: the bitter, icy grip of the frozen lake pulling her under. Her eyelashes fluttered against the dim light, and the sound of crackling fire reached her ears, distant yet comforting.

Her body ached as she tried to move. Her fingers curled into the thick fabric beneath her, something softer than the stone floors of the palace but rougher than the silks she had been accustomed to. A blanket. Slowly, her senses returned, and with them came the sharp realization: she was alive.

Evelyn's eyes finally opened, revealing the wooden beams of a ceiling above her. The air smelled of herbs and something earthy, unfamiliar yet oddly soothing. She turned her head slightly, wincing at the soreness in her neck, and found herself in a small, dimly lit room. A fire burned low in the hearth, casting flickering shadows against the walls. The place was modest, nothing like the grand chambers she had known. Where was she?

Panic threatened to set in, but she forced herself to breathe slowly. Think. The last thing she remembered was the ice beneath her feet cracking. The fall. The darkness. And then... nothing.

A creak at the doorway made her freeze.

She turned her head sharply, her muscles protesting, and found herself staring at a woman—older, with streaks of silver in her dark hair, dressed in a simple woolen gown. The woman's sharp eyes softened slightly upon meeting Evelyn's.

"You're awake," she said, her voice steady, neither harsh nor overly kind. A statement more than anything.

Evelyn swallowed. Her throat felt raw. She wanted to speak, to ask where she was, but her lips wouldn't form the words. She licked them, tasting salt and something bitter.

"Drink this." The woman stepped closer, holding out a wooden cup filled with something steaming. "It will help."

Evelyn paused for a moment, her instincts urging her to be careful, yet her body seemed to have a mind of its own. She was so thirsty, and the aroma wafting from that cup felt inviting and comforting. With shaky hands, she reached out and took a tentative sip. The taste was sharp and bitter, but a soothing warmth enveloped her almost instantly.

The woman watched her, her gaze unreadable. "You should rest more. You've been unconscious for two nights."

Two nights?

Evelyn stiffened, her mind racing. That meant whoever had brought her here had been taking care of her this entire time. But why? And more importantly, who were they?

She swallowed hard. "Where am I?" Her voice was hoarse, barely above a whisper.

The woman exhaled, pulling a stool closer to the bedside. "You're in Brantham. A village beyond the northern hills."

Brantham? Evelyn had never heard of such a place. How far was she from the capital? From her father?

Before she could ask another question, there was a knock at the door. Another figure entered—a man, broad-shouldered with a weathered face. He studied her with cautious eyes, his expression unreadable. Behind him, a younger boy peeked in, curiosity bright in his gaze.

"She's awake?" the man asked gruffly.

"Obviously," the woman replied dryly before turning back to Evelyn. "This is Joren. He was the one who carried you from the lake. And that's Eris. He found you first."

Eris flashed a bright smile at her, but Joren just stood there, completely unfazed.

Evelyn swallowed, gripping the blanket tighter. "I... I don't understand. How did I get here?"

Evelyn swallowed, gripping the blanket tighter. "I... I don't understand. How did I get here?"

Evelyn opened her mouth, then closed it. What was she supposed to say? That she had no memory of how she ended up in this place? That she had fallen through ice and yet somehow survived? The weight of their gazes made her feel uneasy.

"We've never seen anyone like you before," Eris piped up.

"Your clothes, your markings—" he pointed at Evelyn's hands, and for the first time, Evelyn noticed the faint, strange symbols that seemed to have burned onto her skin.

A chill ran through her.

"Do you remember anything?" Siora asked carefully.

Evelyn hesitated. If she told them the truth—that she was the princess, that she had been running from the palace—they might not believe her. Or worse, they might turn her in. She needed to be careful.

"I... don't remember much," she admitted, choosing her words cautiously. "Only that I was running. And then I fell."

Joren narrowed his eyes, as if trying to determine if she was lying. "Running from what?"

Evelyn lowered her gaze. "I... don't know."

A silence stretched between them. The fire crackled softly in the hearth, filling the space where words should have been. Evelyn clenched the blanket around her tighter, uncertainty clawing at her chest.

"Well," Siora finally said, standing. "Whatever happened, you're safe now. Get some rest. We'll talk more later."

Joren seemed like he was itching to dig deeper, but instead, he just nodded sharply and took a step back. Eris hung around for a moment, shooting Evelyn one last curious look before he trailed after them.

Evelyn found herself slipping in and out of sleep, her mind heavy with fatigue and doubt. Each time she shut her eyes, flashes of the icy lake haunted her, the darkness threatening to engulf her completely. And those strange symbols on her hands—what could they possibly signify? Had they always been there? Why was her memory so foggy?

When she opened her eyes again, the room was softly illuminated by a lone lantern. A tray of food rested beside her—rough bread, some broth, and a handful of dried fruits. Her stomach churned with hunger, yet she found herself hesitating. Could she really trust them? But what other options did she have? With trembling hands, she reached for the bread and took a cautious bite.

The door creaked open again. This time, it was Eris.

"You're eating! That's good." He grinned, stepping inside. "Siora was worried you wouldn't."

Evelyn swallowed, studying the boy. He looked no older than sixteen, with an infectious energy about him. There was no fear in his eyes, only curiosity.

"How do you feel?" Eris asked, sitting on the edge of the bed without waiting for permission.

Evelyn hesitated. "Strange."

Eris nodded as if that was the most normal answer. "You're lucky, you know. Most people don't survive falling through ice. Especially not in the dead of winter."

Evelyn frowned. "Lake?"

"Yeah. The ice should have swallowed you whole. But we found you near the edge. Almost like something pushed you out." Eris tilted his head. "Strange, isn't it?"

Evelyn's stomach twisted. Nothing about this made sense.

Eris continued, "Joren doesn't trust you. Thinks you're hiding something."

Evelyn met his gaze. "And you?"

Eris grinned. "I think you're interesting."

CHAPTER TWELVE

THE UNKNOWN GUEST

The village of Brantham was buzzing with a subtle tension, as whispers floated through the chilly morning air. The shocking discovery of the girl—half-frozen and barely clinging to life—had taken over every chat among the villagers. This tight-knit community, which rarely encountered outsiders, suddenly found themselves wrapped up in a mystery that none of them were ready to face.

Eris, the boy who first discovered her, had turned into quite the local sensation, with the elders and his friends eagerly digging for every little detail. As for Joren, the man who rescued the girl from the icy clutches, he hadn't said much about it since. Yet, his silence conveyed so much more than words ever could.

Siora, the village healer, had been caring for the girl who lay unconscious for the last two days. Her home, typically a sanctuary of peace, had become a focal point of whispered curiosity. Having lived a long life, Siora understood the burden of secrets, and it was clear that this girl held more than a few.

"I tell you, it's a bad omen," an old man named Garrik murmured to the small crowd huddled around the village's central well. "You don't just come back from the frozen lake and those marks on her hands—" He quickly made a gesture, as if trying to push away any bad spirits. "Nothing good ever comes from stuff like that."

"A bad omen? Or a blessing?" countered a woman, crossing her arms. "She lived. The ice should have taken her, but it didn't. Perhaps the gods have sent her for a reason."

Joren stood off to the side, taking it all in without saying a word. He couldn't shake the image of the girl's pale face from his mind, nor the way her breath barely moved when they brought her in. But there was something more to her, something that felt off. It wasn't just her survival; it was the mysterious aura surrounding her, like a shadow that refused to let go.

Eris was buzzing with excitement as he brushed aside the elders' superstitions, finding himself hanging around Siora's home, curious about what would unfold next. The girl had finally opened her eyes, and he was the first one to witness it. That moment made him feel like he was part of something much greater than himself.

Inside, Siora watched the girl intently. Even though she seemed weak, her awareness came back surprisingly fast. She had eaten, though she did so with caution, and she listened more than she talked. There was a sense of wariness about her, a protective guard. That was to be expected. Still, Siora had questions—questions that needed to be answered.

When the girl asked where she was, Siora replied, "Brantham, beyond the northern hills." The girl's expression shifted—was it fear? Confusion? Maybe even recognition? It was hard to say for sure. but what truly provoked Siora's curiosity were the strange symbols carved into the girl's hands. They were nothing like anything she had come across before, and considering her years of tending to the injured and exhausted, that was saying something.

The folks here weren't quick to jump to conclusions, but they certainly weren't blind. Whispers circulated like wildfire, with each tale growing more fantastical than the one before. Some said she had plunged from the heavens, while others murmured that she had emerged from the very ice, as if she were reborn.

As the last remnants of daylight faded beyond the hills, the village of Brantham was bathed in the flickering glow of lanterns and hearth fires. A hush had settled over the narrow paths and thatched cottages, broken only by the occasional murmur of conversation or the restless braying of a horse. The air was crisp with the promise of an approaching frost, and the scent of burning wood lingered in the breeze.

Inside Siora's home, Evelyn had finally succumbed to sleep, her breathing steady but her brow furrowed, as if her dreams held echoes of a past she could not yet piece together. The healer sat nearby, watching over the girl with a quiet intensity. She had tended to many over the years, but never had she felt such an unshakable sense of unease about a patient. The markings on the girl's hands seemed almost to pulse under the dim candlelight, and Siora could not deny that the weight of mystery around the girl was growing heavier by the hour.

Outside, the villagers were still awake, not quite ready to call it a night. In the clearing by the ancient oak tree at the center of the village, a small group had gathered, their voices low but filled with urgency. Joren stood there, arms crossed, his keen eyes scanning the faces around him. He had witnessed fear in men's eyes before, but there was something unsettling about the way the villagers kept glancing toward Siora's home, as if they were bracing for something unnatural to unfold at any moment

"The girl hasn't mentioned where she came from," Garrik said quietly, gripping his walking staff a little tighter. "And what about those symbols? You don't see a regular traveler with markings like those."

"Maybe she just doesn't remember," a younger man said, warming his hands together. "We tend to jump to conclusions too quickly. After all, she's just a girl."

"A girl who should not be alive," another man countered. "You all know what the frozen waters do. No one has ever fallen through and lived."

Eris, who had been hanging back during the conversation, finally decided to step in. "Look, she's not a monster or anything. She's just like us—maybe a little lost, maybe a bit scared. But honestly, I don't think we should treat her like she's some kind of bad omen."

Garrik let out a snort. "Sounds like something a boy would say, someone who hasn't yet felt the burden of the unknown."

Joren, who had been silent thus far, finally spoke. "Enough. We know too little to make claims. Let the girl rest. We will have our answers in time."

The villagers murmured their discontent but gradually started to scatter. Yet, a sense of unease hung in the air. It wasn't Evelyn herself that frightened them—it was the uncertainty of what her arrival could mean. Old superstitions floated around, tales of caution shared through the ages. A stranger pulled from the ice—what if she was never meant to be rescued? What if something worse was on its way for her?

As the night deepened, the village's usual peace felt fragile, as though something unseen was pressing against the very fabric of their quiet world. Siora remained at Evelyn's bedside, listening to the wind rattle the wooden beams of her cottage, listening to the girl's breath, slow and steady. There was something stirring in Brantham, something beyond their understanding

Change had already arrived, whether they wanted it to or not.

CHAPTER THIRTEEN

A Glow in the Dark

Evelyn sat on the edge of the wooden cot, staring at her hands. The markings on her skin, the strange symbols she did not recognize, seemed to pulse softly in the flickering candlelight. It had been over a day since she arrived in Brantham, yet the sense of being out of place only intensified. The villagers had welcomed her, shared their names, and explained her surroundings, but none of it answered the questions that clawed at her mind. Where had she come from? What had led her to that frozen lake? And why, despite everything, did she have this nagging feeling that something essential was just out of reach?

She lct out a long, slow breath, her fingers gently gliding over the textured wooden frame beneath her. Siora had been a true blessing, taking care of her wounds and providing her with warm meals and comforting words. Unlike the others, Eris was the only one who really treated her like she belonged, as if she were more than just a strange presence to be feared. Joren, while cautious, at least looked at her with a sense of reason. As for the rest of the village? They observed her with a quiet unease, almost as if they were just waiting for her to confirm their doubts.

Evelyn pulled the blanket tighter around her shoulders. The cottage was small but warm, a fire crackling in the hearth, casting golden shadows across the stone walls. She had not ventured outside much yet—only once to see the village square, where people bustled about their daily routines, though their eyes never stopped glancing in her direction.

A knock at the door made her tense. Before she could respond, Siora pushed it open and stepped inside, carrying a wooden tray with a bowl of stew and a slice of bread. "You need to eat more," the healer said, setting it down beside her.

Evelyn hesitated before picking up the spoon. "Thank you," she murmured, her voice quieter than she intended.

Siora studied her, arms crossed. "You've been lost in thought since morning. I imagine it's a lot to take in."

Evelyn swallowed a spoonful of the warm broth before speaking. "I don't understand why I can't remember. I know my name. I know how to speak, how to think. But everything before waking up here is... blank. I don't even know why I was in that lake."

Siora sighed, sitting down in the chair opposite her. "Memories are strange things. Some return in time. Others remain hidden until they're forced to the surface."

"And if they never return?" Evelyn's fingers tightened around the spoon. "What if I never remember who I am?"

Before Siora could respond, another knock came at the door—firmer this time. Joren entered, his expression unreadable. "Eris wants to take Evelyn outside. Thought it might do her good to see more of the village."

Evelyn glanced at Siora, who gave a small nod. She wasn't sure if she was ready to face the people's stares again, but staying locked away wouldn't bring her any closer to answers.

Joren stepped aside as she walked toward the door, the cool evening air greeting her as she stepped outside. Eris stood a few steps away, waiting with an eager expression. "You've been stuck in there too long. Come on, let's walk."

She followed him through the village, the dirt paths winding between stone cottages and small wooden fences. The villagers watched but said nothing as she passed. It was unsettling, this silent judgment, but she forced herself to ignore it.

"They'll come around," Eris said, as if reading her thoughts. "You just need to show them you're not a threat."

"And how do I do that?" she asked, glancing at him.

He grinned. "Start by not looking so terrified all the time."

Evelyn let out a huff, but a small smile crept onto her face. For the first time since she had woken up in this strange place, she felt a hint of normalcy wash over her.

They walked until they reached the outskirts of the village, where a small grassy clearing overlooked a still pond, its surface reflecting the pale light of the evening sun. Eris sat down on a fallen log and patted the space beside him. "Sit."

Evelyn hesitated before lowering herself onto the log, pulling her cloak tighter around her. The air was cool, the distant sounds of the village fading into the quiet hum of nature.

"You look like you have a thousand thoughts running through your head," Eris said, leaning back on his hands. "Want to share any of them?"

She let out a slow breath. "I just... I feel like I'm trapped between two places. I woke up here, and this is all I know

now. But there's something else—something I can't reach."

Eris was silent for a moment before saying, "Maybe you're not supposed to reach it just yet. Maybe it's something that'll come when it's ready."

"But what if I need it now?" she asked, staring at her hands again. "What if my past has the answers I need?"

He studied her for a moment. "Maybe. But have you considered that your past might not be something you want to remember?"

Evelyn swallowed hard. The thought had crossed her mind, but she had refused to entertain it. What if she had been running from something? What if the reason she had ended up in that lake was because she had no choice?

"I don't know what's worse," she admitted, her voice barely above a whisper. "Not knowing who I am or being afraid of what I might find out."

Eris sighed and leaned forward, resting his elbows on his knees. "Look, I don't have answers for you. But I do know this—right now, you're here. You're alive. That has to count for something."

She turned to him, her expression softening. "Why are you being so kind to me? The others don't trust me. Even Joren seems a bit on edge around me."

He shrugged. "I don't know. Maybe because I've always believed that things happen for a reason. You ended up here, of all places. That has to mean something, right?"

Evelyn looked out at the pond, watching the way the water rippled under the night breeze. Maybe he was right. Maybe she had to stop chasing the past and start figuring out how to live in the present.

Before she could answer, a sudden warmth spread across her hands. Evelyn looked down in alarm as the strange markings on her skin glowed softly, their intricate symbols shifting, almost as if they were alive. She gasped, her breath catching in her throat. The glow pulsed faintly, illuminating the dim evening light.

Eris stared, eyes widening. "What the—"

"It's happening,"Siora's voice interrupted them. She had appeared behind them, her gaze locked onto Evelyn's hands.

"It's happening," she murmured. "The markings... they've awakened."

Evelyn's breath came in shallow gasps. "What does this mean? Why is this happening to me?"

Siora took a deep breath. "To you. Because you are the chosen one."

Evelyn's heartbeat quickened. "Chosen? For what?"

Siora stepped closer, her gaze never leaving the glowing sigils. "BEvelyn... you were never just anyone. These markings—this power—it's waking up because it has found its bearer."

Evelyn shook her head. "Bearer of what? What am I supposed to do?"

Siora's expression was unreadable, yet her voice carried weight. "That is the question, isn't it? The world has been waiting for you, Evelyn. But whether that is a blessing or a curse... remains to be seen."

CHAPTER FOURTEEN

THE WEIGHT OF KNOWING

Evelyn sat alone in Siora's cottage, her gaze fixed on the symbols that had etched themselves into her memory just as deeply as they had onto her skin. The radiant glow had long since dimmed, leaving an unsettling silence behind, yet she could still sense something stirring within her, coming to life. A presence. A purpose. It was something she didn't fully grasp yet, but it was impossible to ignore any longer.

She tightened her fists, a wave of frustration building up inside her. The markings had responded to something—what exactly, she couldn't say. And Siora had gazed at her with such intensity that it made her feel vulnerable, as if she were more than just herself, something... meant for a greater purpose. But meant for what?

A gentle knock at the door snapped her out of her thoughts. Just as she was about to respond, Siora walked in, clutching an ancient leather-bound book. Her face was a mystery, but there was something heavy in her gaze that made Evelyn's heart race.

"I suppose you have questions," Siora said, setting the book down on the wooden table between them.

Evelyn rolled her eyes. "That's putting it mildly." She waved her hands in the air. "What's going on with me? Why do I have these? And why does it feel like... like something is stirring inside me?"

Siora exhaled slowly, as if she had been waiting for this moment for a long time. "Because, child, you were never meant to be ordinary. You were chosen long before you ever set foot in Brantham."

Evelyn's stomach twisted. "Chosen for what?"

Siora paused for a brief moment, taking a deep breath before she finally opened the book. The pages had turned a yellowish hue over the years, and though the ink had faded, it was still readable. Evelyn leaned closer, her heart racing as she spotted the symbols on the parchment—symbols that looked just like the ones etched on her own skin.

"This is the Book of the Lost Symbols," Siora explained. "It tells the tale of an ancient power—something that has only been held by a select few throughout the ages. They were called the Marked."

"The Marked," Evelyn repeated, the words foreign and yet strangely familiar.

Siora nodded. "Their purpose was to act as the balance between forces we barely understand. To restore, to protect... or, in some cases, to destroy."

Evelyn's throat tightened. "And you think I'm one of them?"

"There is no thinking," Siora said firmly. "You are. The markings appeared on you, not by chance, but because the time has come for their bearer to rise again."

Evelyn shook her head. "But I don't remember anything about this. How could I be tied to something I know nothing about?"

"Because the Marked have always been lost before they are found," Siora murmured, her voice laced with something close to sorrow. "It is part of the cycle. A test, if you will. Their memories are often stripped away before they are ready, so they must seek their truth on their own."

Siora reached across the table, placing a gentle hand over Evelyn's. "Your past is hidden from you because it is not yet time for you to claim it. But the markings waking up? That means the time is drawing near."

Evelyn pulled her hands back, standing abruptly. She paced the room, her mind spinning. "This doesn't make sense. If I was chosen for something—if I was supposed to have these—why would I end up in a frozen lake? Why wouldn't I remember anything?"

Siora watched her carefully. "Perhaps you were meant to die that day. Perhaps someone knew what you were and tried to erase you before you could awaken."

Evelyn stopped mid-step, her breath catching. The thought chilled her to the bone. "You mean someone tried to kill me?"

"I do not know for certain," Siora admitted. "But what I do know is that the power you bear is not something all would welcome. The Marked have always had enemies, those who fear what they could do."

Evelyn felt a hollow weight settle in her chest. "Then... what am I supposed to do?"

Siora closed the book, meeting Evelyn's gaze with quiet resolve. "That is for you to decide. You may seek out the truth of who you are, or you may turn away from it. But know this, child—your power has awoken. And whether you accept it or not, others will come searching for it."

A shiver ran through Evelyn, but she forced herself to stand taller. She had spent days questioning who she was, where she had come from. But now, for the first time, she realized the real question was not who she had been—but who she was meant to become.

In the days that followed, Evelyn remained near the village, quietly observing, listening, and soaking in everything around her. The villagers, who had once been wary, now acknowledged her with nods and soft-spoken words, their eyes reflecting a blend of respect and doubt.

Rumors flew around Brantham like a raging fire—talk of the girl with the mysterious ancient marks, a stranger who somehow survived when she should have perished.

Evelyn spent her mornings wandering the edges of the village and her evenings in quiet talks with Siora, asking questions that often led to more riddles. But she was beginning to understand. Not just who she might be, but what her existence meant.

Evelyn discovered the different realms: the world of humans, the mysterious Otherworld wrapped in legends, and the Veiled Realm—an ancient, fragmented space that lies between worlds. The markings on her hands weren't just symbols; they were keys. Not to physical doors, but to deep truths that had been hidden for ages. As she delved into this knowledge, she began to unravel parts of a much bigger tapestry, and before she knew it, she was caught up in its intricate threads.

One evening, as the sun sank behind the rugged peaks beyond Brantham, Evelyn found herself sitting next to the gentle stream that curved its way around the village. The water sparkled like gold, and a soft breeze rustled through the trees. She ran her fingers along the lines of her palm, the patterns standing out even in the fading light.

Siora approached quietly, settling beside her.

"They're changing," Evelyn murmured.

"Yes," Siora replied. "Because you are."

"Why me?" Evelyn asked. "Why not someone stronger? Someone who knew what they were getting into?"

Siora took a moment before responding. When she finally spoke, her tone was gentler than normal. "It's because the prediction talks about a child born from two worlds. Someone who can walk between them and mend what has been broken."

Evelyn looked at her, startled. "Two realms?"

Siora nodded. "You are not just of this world, Evelyn. And your father—he knew. He knew what you were destined to become. That's why he feared you."

A cold realization bloomed in Evelyn's chest. "He knew the markings would come."

"He did," Siora said. "But he hoped to stop them. He tried to shape fate through control. But fate doesn't bend easily."

Evelyn was quiet for a long time. "He didn't want to protect me. He wanted to prevent this."

Siora placed a hand on her shoulder. "And now the choice lies with you. The markings have awakened—but the reason why... that truth is still waiting."

The wind shifted. In the distance, bells rang faintly from the watchtower, a signal of someone approaching. Evelyn turned her gaze to the horizon, heart thudding.

She didn't know who would come. But she knew one thing: the next answers would not come easily. They would have to be earned, perhaps even fought for. And she was ready to begin.

CHAPTER FIFTEEN

TRUTHS BEHIND THE VEIL

The days were getting chillier, but nothing compared to the icy determination building within Evelyn. Her nights were filled with restlessness, haunted by fragmented visions—her father's face, not radiating warmth but filled with fear; shadowy figures slipping through beams of light; and an ancient voice echoing from deep below the earth. All these signs hinted at a truth she had yet to fully grasp.

Early that morning, Siora guided Evelyn away from the familiar village paths and into the woods, leading her beyond the frost covered trees to a place that was entirely new to her. The underbrush transformed into a carpet of mossy stones and twisting roots, eventually opening up to a serene clearing enveloped in quiet. At the heart of this clearing stood a shrine, ancient and seemingly cradled by the forest itself. Weathered stone columns encircled a circular platform, adorned with runes that glimmered softly in Evelyn's presence.

"This is where the first of the Marked were guided," Siora said softly, stepping aside so Evelyn could approach. "It's hidden even from most of the village. But I think it's time you see it."

As Evelyn stepped onto the platform, the markings on her skin warmed—softly at first, then brighter, responding to the energy held within the stones. She could feel something stir, not within the shrine, but within herself.

The shrine didn't offer answers outright. But it affirmed one thing: she was not imagining her purpose.

The morning after her visit to the shrine, Evelyn stood atop a ridge overlooking the village of Brantham, the sun cresting just over the horizon. She had asked to be left alone. Her thoughts needed space. But today wasn't just for reflection. It was for preparation.

That very night, as the sun dipped below the horizon and painted the sky in shades of twilight, something extraordinary happened—a celestial alignment that had been spoken of in ancient writings and dreaded in long-lost prophecies. The stars twinkled with an unusual brilliance, and the atmosphere felt alive with a mysterious energy. A glowing ribbon stretched across the sky, delicate as silk yet brimming with an undeniable force.

Siora's face turned grave as she watched the heavens. "The veil between realms is thinning," she murmured. "It hasn't done so in over a hundred years."

Evelyn stood beside her, the faint glow from her markings intensifying. "What does it mean?"

"It means," Siora replied, "if you're going to cross into the Other Realm, this may be the only chance you'll have."

Without a moment's pause, Evelyn called upon her most trusted friends—Eris, who was always by her side, and Joren, the one whose expertise in paths and maps was absolutely crucial. The three of them set to work, gathering supplies, protection charms, and seeking Siora's wisdom to help them locate the threshold.

By lantern-light, the villagers watched them from a respectful distance—some wary, others filled with cautious hope. The girl with the markings, the one whispered to be chosen, was about to walk where no villager had dared for generations.

The three friends set off beneath the soft glow of the night sky. The forest was eerily quiet, as if the air itself was holding its breath. Each branch they brushed against appeared to pull back slightly, and the mist seemed to wrap around itself a bit more tightly, almost hesitant to see what was about to happen.

Siora guided them until they reached a place where the trees arched overhead in an impossible curve, forming a living gateway. At its base, stones circled a pool of dark water that reflected not the stars, but strange constellations unfamiliar to any sky they knew.

"This is it," Siora said. "The threshold. Once you step through, the way back may not be the same."

Evelyn glanced at Eris and Joren. Neither flinched. They were ready.

As she stepped into the circle, her markings ignited in response—no longer just warm or faintly glowing, but pulsing, like the beat of a second heart. Light spilled from her palms, spiraling out into the air, pulling on the veil like wind on silk. The pool rippled, then shimmered, its surface becoming mirror-smooth—and then it broke apart like glass, revealing a void beneath.

She didn't hesitate.

The sensation was like falling, but without motion. Like holding your breath in a dream and suddenly realizing you'd never exhaled. The cold of the realm hit first—not frost on skin, but in the soul. And then color. Color like nothing they'd seen before: bleeding purples and emerald greens that twisted in the sky like smoke; trees with silver bark that whispered secrets in foreign tongues.

They had arrived in the Veiled Realm.

The land itself felt alive, conscious. Trails didn't stay in one place. Light moved independently of any sun. Sounds echoed wrong—too slow, or too fast. Joren was the first to realize they were being watched, not by creatures or beasts, but by the realm itself.

"It's testing us," he whispered.

Eris knelt by a flower whose petals folded inward as his fingers approached. "Or warning us."

The deeper they walked, the more Evelyn felt something stir inside her—not just the markings, but memories that weren't hers. Images of past bearers of the mark. Of battles fought at the edges of time. Of gates sealed and names forgotten.

In a secluded grove draped in hanging vines, they stumbled upon the remains of an ancient structure—twisted stone columns that seemed to be slowly reclaimed by the bizarre plants of the area. It pulsed softly, echoing the same rhythm as Evelyn's markings.

Joren translated what little script remained: "From the blood of two, the bearer shall rise. Balance, once broken, must be restored."

"The blood of two?" Eris asked.

Evelyn's breath caught in her throat. The king... and someone else. Her mother?

That night, they made camp under a canopy of stars that weren't stars at all, but glowing orbs that floated lazily through the sky. Evelyn couldn't sleep. She stood alone, staring into the depths of a glimmering stream that reflected memories instead of faces.

In its shifting surface, she saw her father—King Aldric—standing over a map. A younger version of him, with the same cold resolve she now recognized. He wasn't planning war.

He was preparing a sealing.

He knew the realms would align again.

He knew the child born of the queen would be the only one capable of reopening the path—and he had sworn to stop that from ever happening.

Not out of protection.

But out of fear.

Evelyn took a step back, her heart racing. This wasn't just about fate for her; it felt like she was being played. Her very existence was a prophecy come to life, but it had been kept in the shadows, stifled, and controlled.

When she returned to the camp, Joren was waiting—his figure emerging like shadow from the trees.

"You saw it, didn't you?" Joren said softly.

"I saw enough."

"Then you understand now. The realms were never meant to be separate. They were torn apart by men in power, afraid of what unity would bring."

"And I'm meant to fix that?" Evelyn's voice was barely a whisper. "What if I can't?"

Joren placed a hand on her shoulder. "It's not about what you can or can't do. It's about what you choose to do—now that you know."

Evelyn turned her gaze to the eerie horizon of the Veiled Realm, where the land shifted like thought and the sky never stayed still. She didn't have all the answers. But the truth had been set in motion.

And she would follow it—through whatever this realm held.

Through betrayal.

Through light and shadow.

To the end.

Days passed since their return from the Veiled Realm. Life in Brantham resumed its quiet rhythms, but Evelyn felt like she moved through it in echoes. Her thoughts constantly returned to the visions she'd seen, the truths unearthed, and the sense that something—someone—was still withholding a final piece of the puzzle.

It came one morning wrapped in simple parchment, tucked between pages of an old book delivered by a traveling merchant. She opened it idly at first, until her eyes caught the handwriting.

Her father's.

The letter was dated months before her disappearance—a time when she had still lived in the comfort of the palace, unaware of what fate awaited her.

My dearest Evelyn,

If this reaches you, then fate has done what I feared it might. I do not know where you are or who will place this letter in your hands, only that I prayed you would never read it.

There are things I should have told you long ago. Things no father wants to lay at the feet of his daughter. The day you were born, the stars shifted. The markings you now bear were foretold, not born with you, but waiting to awaken.

I tried to stop it. Not out of hatred, but out of fear. Fear of what your role would demand. Fear of the Veiled King and his hunger for dominion. I made choices—choices I now regret.

If you are reading this, you must now know the truth. Not all lies are spoken; some are lived. I cloaked you in safety to keep you from the fire, but perhaps you were always meant to walk through it.

Forgive me if you can.

The parchment trembled in Evelyn's hands. Her chest felt hollow, as though something vital had been scooped out from inside her.

These were not the words of a man protecting his daughter. These were the confessions of a king who had acted out of fear—not just for her, but of her. She could feel it in every line, between every carefully chosen word. Though he claimed to have acted from dread of the Veiled King, it was clear to her now: Aldric feared her power most of all.

He feared what she represented.

He feared what she might choose to become.

And so, instead of raising her to face that destiny, he had tried to contain her, to clip the wings before she learned to fly. Not because he didn't care, but because he cared more for the order he had built. His actions weren't born of paternal love—they were rooted in self-preservation.

The betrayal stung sharper than any blade. Evelyn's entire life, she had searched for purpose, for belonging. And now she saw that the path had been buried beneath lies, not to protect her, but to protect the fragile legacy of a man who couldn't bear to see her outgrow him.

Her hands curled into fists, the markings on her skin flaring faintly in response to the storm within her.

She no longer needed her father's approval. She no longer needed anyone's permission.

The truth was hers now.

CHAPTER SIXTEEN

THE EMPTY THRONE

The air had grown noticeably colder as the weeks passed, but it wasn't just the chill that had Brantham buzzing in hushed tones—it was the quiet revolution blooming in its shadows.

Evelyn was different now that she was back from the Veiled Realm. There was a new brightness in her eyes, as if the fog of doubt had been cleared away by the truth she now held. But this clarity didn't bring her peace; instead, it brought her choices. And Evelyn had made her decision.

Evelyn started to gather her most trusted allies—Eris, Joren, and a handful of villagers who hadn't let fear sway their loyalty. They convened under the old storehouse as night fell, its sturdy stone foundation standing strong, with the entrance cleverly concealed under mounds of hay. The lanterns were turned down low, their flames just barely dancing against the glass, casting soft flickers of light across their faces as Evelyn began to speak.

"I've glimpsed what's beyond the Veil," she started, standing tall in the middle, her markings softly glowing in the dim light. "These realms were never meant to be torn apart. We were split by kings who were afraid of what true unity would require. My father was one of those kings."

Gasps moved through the room, but no one interrupted. Eris sat forward, his hands folded, while Joren watched Evelyn with steady eyes.

She held up the letter. "He feared the power of the Veiled King, yes. But more than that—he feared me. He feared what I might do if I stepped into who I was meant to be."

Silence followed. Then Joren spoke, voice low. "What do you plan to do now?"

"I will return," she said, her voice a blade. "Not to reclaim a throne—but to speak truth in the very heart of his court. The time for secrets is over."

A murmur of both dread and admiration spread through the room. One villager, a quiet elder named Thessa, looked up. "He will not let you walk out freely once you've shown your hand."

"Then I won't walk out," Evelyn said. "I'll rise above."

Thessa stood slowly, her eyes fixed on Evelyn with an emotion somewhere between awe and sorrow. "Do you understand what you're doing, child? Kings don't bend to truth. They crush it."

Evelyn met her gaze. "Then I'll be the truth that refuses to break."

Thessa stepped closer, placing a hand on Evelyn's arm. "You're not just threatening a crown. You're unraveling history. But... if you truly mean to do this, you won't be alone. Not anymore."

The soft murmur of agreement from others in the room was like wind rustling through trees—quiet but gathering force.

They prepared for three days. Joren charted safe routes into the capital while Eris forged documents and arranged disguises. Evelyn cut her hair, tied it back in the style of the lower court, and wore a traveling cloak that dimmed the light of her markings. Her presence would cause alarm, so they would enter through the servant's passage—a forgotten corridor buried beneath the palace gardens.

But that wasn't the only path they needed to chart.

Crossing the realms again would not be as simple. With the veil's realm still shaky from their last adventure, Evelyn had to figure out a safe passage—one that would not only let her return to the Veiled Realm but also potentially bring others along in the future. She decided to seek out one of the old Keepers of Lore in Brantham, a blind man named Coren. He spoke of an ancient convergence point hidden beneath the ruins of an old temple at the edge of the woods.

"There's a hidden passage right there," Coren said, his voice rasping like dry leaves. "A path older than the divide. It hasn't been opened in decades—not since the realms were sealed. But if the symbols on your hand truly are what I believe, you might just have the key."

With Joren by her side, Evelyn traced ancient maps and explored secret tunnels, crafting a backup route in case she needed to shift between realms in a hurry. They marked the trees and left cryptic messages etched in stone. The journey towards unity wasn't solely about politics—it was about knowledge, careful planning, and the rediscovery of ancient magic that had been forgotten for ages

With the passage secured and the path to the capital mapped, Evelyn turned her attention to the next step: confronting her father.

The journey unfolded in silence. Fields gradually gave way to dense forests, which then transformed into rugged stone roads. As twilight descended, the grand gates of the kingdom rose before her. Once she stepped inside, Evelyn sensed a visible shift in the atmosphere—an awareness, heavy with the feeling of unseen eyes upon her. The palace remained the same, but she had changed in ways she could hardly comprehend.

They quietly made their way through a secret passage that lay beneath a weathered marble lion. Joren lingered back to keep an eye on their escape route. Eris ventured forward to scout the corridor, while Evelyn glided like a wisp of smoke, stealthy and determined, heading toward the hall where her father still held power.

The throne room was still when she walked in. Grand tapestries hung from the walls, and moonlight streamed through the stained glass, casting beautiful patterns of violet and gold on the floor. King Aldric stood by the large window, his hands clasped behind his back, lost in thought.

He did not turn.

"I wondered how long it would take," he said.

Evelyn stepped forward. "You knew I'd come?"

"You were always more your mother's daughter than mine," he said. "Curious. Unyielding."

"She would've told me the truth."

A pause.

Aldric finally turned, his face more worn than she remembered, but no less cold. "Truth is a weapon, Evelyn. And sometimes it wounds too deeply to wield."

"That's why you hid it? Because it was easier to live behind walls than to face what unity might bring?"

He stepped toward her, regal and proud. "I did what was necessary to protect the balance. To protect you."

"No," she said, her voice unwavering. "You protected your reign. You clipped my wings so I'd never learn to fly—and you call that love."

A flicker of something—regret?—passed across his face. But he did not deny it.

"You were always meant for something greater," he said quietly.

"Then let me be it," Evelyn replied. "But not under your crown."

By dawn, the city had stirred with rumors. The Princess had returned. She had entered the throne room. She had survived the Veiled Realm.

That morning, Evelyn found herself standing on the marble dais in the heart of the capital's square. A diverse crowd had come together—nobles, merchants, and villagers all mingling. Her cloak was gone, and as the gentle morning light bathed her, her markings shimmered. Her voice resonated with a profound sense of revelation.

"People of the realm," she began. "You have been kept in darkness. Told the realms beyond our borders were wild, dangerous. That we must remain divided to stay safe. But I have seen the truth. And I will no longer serve a lie."

Gasps and murmurs rippled outward. Aldric did not appear.

"I am not here to claim the crown. I am no longer your heir. I renounce my place, not out of rebellion—but out of hope. Hope that we can build something greater. That the time of fear is over."

She raised her hand, the light from her markings casting arcs across the sky.

"The realms can be reunited. And I will walk the path to that future—even if I must do it alone."

But as she turned from the dais, she saw faces turning toward her—not away.

That night, Eris and Joren remained hidden in the lower servant quarters beneath the palace, disguised with forged documents. The cramped stone walls and flickering torches provided little comfort, but the proximity to Evelyn—and their readiness was all that mattered.

She would not be walking alone.

CHAPTER SEVENTEEN

ASHES OF THE CROWN

The days that followed Evelyn's renunciation were thick with silence—not the peace of stillness, but the kind that comes before a storm.

Whispers traveled faster than the city's wind. Some hailed her as a beacon of change, others called her a traitor. But Evelyn did not retreat. Instead, she moved quietly through the stone halls of the capital, not as a princess, but as something else—something unshaped and still becoming.

She didn't bother with guards. There was no court to preside over. The once vibrant golden threads of her royal attire had vanished, now swapped for more subdued fabrics, with the soft glow of her symbols pulsing steadily like a second heartbeat.

From the shadows, spies watched her. Ministers sent letters back and forth behind closed doors. The throne remained cold, as King Aldric refused to appear publicly. The people took this for weakness. Evelyn knew it was fear.

She met each night with Eris and Joren in the underground corners of the palace. Maps were unfolded.

Letters drafted. Plans whispered.

"The court will fracture soon," Joren said one evening, voice low. "Many are waiting to see where the wind turns."

"It has already turned," Evelyn said. "They just don't know it yet."

In the villages, a different kind of buzz was in the air—whispers about the border towns becoming uneasy. Traders were sharing tales of shadowy figures lurking just beyond the forests, observing and biding their time. It felt as if the Veiled Realm was no longer satisfied with remaining in the shadows.

And then, the letter arrived. Not addressed to Evelyn, but to Thessa. Carried by a cloaked messenger who vanished the moment it changed hands. The seal was foreign—neither Aldric's nor any known noble house.

Inside, a single line written in fine ink:

The king's silence is not surrender. Be wary—he does not forget betrayal, not even from blood.

That night, Evelyn found herself standing on the palace tower, gazing out at the city that had once been her home. The lights twinkled below, resembling stars that had tumbled down to the earth.

"He's watching me," she murmured.

Eris, standing beside her, nodded. "Let him. You've already stepped beyond him."

But Evelyn wasn't certain. Not yet.

Her war wasn't with the crown.

It was with the history written beneath it.

The next morning, Evelyn stepped into the old war chamber, a place that had been gathering dust for years. The ironwood table still bore the faint marks of battles that had long since faded into history. She carefully unrolled a new scroll across its surface, her fingers gliding along the edges that once defined the boundaries between realms.

"We need to speak to the outland settlements," she told Joren and Eris. "If we can get them to see the truth, the rest will follow."

"That won't be easy," Eris said. "They've been raised to fear the Veiled Realm."

"So was I," Evelyn answered. "But fear only has power if you feed it. It's time we give them something else."

They dedicated hours to putting together a list of reliable messengers—people who truly believed in Evelyn's mission and could move around without drawing attention. It was like a council of watchful eyes and ears, ready to spread the message of unity without causing any panic. By the flickering light of candles, they penned hidden letters, sealing them with Evelyn's unique mark—a symbol she had crafted herself, inspired by the designs of her radiant symbols: a sun split into three arcs, each one symbolizing a different realm, all converging toward a single center.

It was not a symbol of royalty. It was a symbol of convergence.

In the days that followed, Evelyn met with nobles who had once served her father. Some turned her away with closed doors and thin smiles. But others listened—especially those who had lost family to the realm conflicts.

"If the realms come together," she said to one countess, her eyes filled with sorrow, "we won't lose any more children to the mist. No more weapons will be drawn out of fear."

She did not promise peace. She promised truth. And it was enough for some to turn their gaze toward her.

The weight still felt heavy on her shoulders. In the stillness of the night, when the palace fell silent, Evelyn sat in the old observatory alone. The stars, once filled with stories, now seemed more like watchful eyes keeping an eye on her.

"You would've understood," she whispered to the memory of her mother. "You would've stood beside me."

Footsteps interrupted her silence. Joren appeared in the doorway, his expression unreadable.

"There's movement on the eastern road," he said. "Scouts from your father's guard. Small company. They may be coming for you."

Evelyn stood. Her voice was steady.

"Let them come. I'm done hiding."

SECRETS OF THE VEIL

The Veiled Realm was not a place—it was a sensation.

The mist wrapped around their clothes like the gentle exhale of a sleeping creature. The trees loomed silently, their gnarled trunks marked with symbols that predate written history. Evelyn moved forward, her fingers brushing against the bark, her sigils softly glowing in reply. With each step further into the forest, it felt as if she was walking through a memory.

Joren moved like a shadow behind her, quiet but alert. Eris, ever curious, paused at every glint of light or flutter of wings. "This place watches us," he murmured once. Evelyn didn't disagree.

They were guided not by map, but by instinct—the pull of her markings, a warmth beneath her skin that grew stronger with each step they took. Siora had cautioned her: the Veiled Realm uncovers truths, but it doesn't always do so kindly.

After what felt like hours of winding through the forest, the mist finally thinned out just enough to unveil a hidden gem: a clearing that seemed completely untouched by time.

Right in the middle, there was a stone monolith, partially covered in vines, etched with the same spiral patterns that adorned Evelyn's palms. As she drew closer, her symbols began to glow more intensely, pulsing rhythmically like a heartbeat.

Joren unslung his blade. "It's reacting to you."

She touched the stone. It trembled under her fingers—and then, it sang.

A deep, echoing sound, almost like a hidden chorus beneath the earth, filled the air. The wind howled as it whipped through the trees. Below their feet, the ground shimmered and shifted, creating an unsettling atmosphere.

The forest blurred. Trees twisted, reshaping. The stone sank into the earth. In its place rose a staircase—spiraling downward, into the dark.

"What is this?" Eris whispered.

"A gate," Evelyn said softly. "Or a memory."

They descended.

What lay beneath wasn't destruction, but rather a careful preservation. It was a hall sculpted from obsidian and moonstone, illuminated by orbs that drifted like quiet stars. The walls were adorned with frescoes that told the tale of a world that was once complete—three realms intricately woven together, united by light. That is, until one—cloaked in shadow—snapped the threads apart.

The Veiled King.

Beneath one mural, Evelyn found an inscription in ancient runes. Joren read them aloud, voice echoing in the silence:

"The one who bears the tri-marked flame shall mend what was sundered—or burn in its wake."

Evelyn stared at her hands. The markings glowed fiercely now.

"This was never just about me," she said.

"No," Joren said. "It never was."

Just then, a sudden gust of wind rushed through the chamber, even though no door was open. The orbs hanging above flickered to life, and the murals seemed to quiver. From further down the hall, footsteps echoed—steady and purposeful.

Eris tensed. Joren drew his blade.

Out from the dimly lit archway emerged a figure cloaked in flowing layers of robes, their face concealed behind a mask made of reflective glass.

"You shouldn't be here," the figure said. The voice was neither male nor female—but both, echoing as though layered in time.

Evelyn met the masked gaze, heart pounding.

"I'm here for answers."

The figure tilted its head. "Then prepare for a truth that might unmake you."

The lights went out.

Darkness swallowed everything.

For a brief moment, Evelyn felt like she couldn't catch her breath. The sudden darkness enveloped her, pressing down like an unyielding weight. She could hear Eris's breath quickening next to her and sensed Joren shifting his position slightly. The figure in the mirror remained still, not a single movement.

Then a single orb flickered back to life, hovering between Evelyn and the stranger. Its glow was dim, casting long, eerie shadows on the obsidian floor.

"Truth," the masked figure repeated, voice like layered whispers, "is not a comfort. It is a blade."

"Then give it to me," Evelyn said. "I've already been cut open by lies."

The figure stepped forward, the soft rustle of robes echoing like a breeze in an empty temple. "Very well."

With a smooth movement, the figure raised a hand, and from the emptiness above, symbols burst into light. They whirled in the air: glyphs of realms, of harmony, of treachery. Evelyn's symbols started to glow in rhythm with them.

"The Veiled Realm," the stranger began, "didn't come into existence because of exile. It was created through a deliberate choice. A choice made by your father, Aldric of the Crowned Realm, when he became wary of a prophecy—one that echoed through ancient stones and the light of stars. It foretold of a chosen soul destined to reunite the realms. Not to conquer, but to heal."

Eris let out a breath. Joren tightened his grip on his sword.

"He believed unity would undo his rule. So he sought the prophecy, stole the texts from the Veiled archives, and twisted them. He spread lies among the other realms. When our king refused to submit or forget, Aldric and his allies cast the Veil itself—sealing away not just land, but knowledge."

The figure paused, and their tone deepened. "But it was not fear alone. Aldric had tasted dominance—had stood above others too long to ever step down willingly. He saw the power the prophecy promised, and he did not want to share it. Not with the Veiled King. Not with anyone. Especially not with a child who might one day outshine him."

Evelyn's voice cracked. "He sealed the prophecy?"

The figure nodded. "He feared it would lead to you. So he erased it from the world—except for the fragments hidden here."

The masked figure added. "And so, he helped create the Veil—an eternal barrier. One meant to contain not just our king, but the truth itself."

The floating glyphs began to pulse faster. Behind them, the murals shifted again—showing Aldric standing beside others, their hands raised, casting a spell that fractured the world.

"He told me he was protecting me," Evelyn whispered. "But he was protecting his rule."

The mirrored mask shifted to face her. "And now, the threads begin to unravel. The realms are awakening. The Veil is growing thin. You are the fulcrum."

"What do I have to do?" Evelyn asked, her voice steadier than she felt.

"You must choose. Rejoin what was severed... or preserve the lie."

Joren stepped forward, his voice low but firm. "And what does that mean for your king? For the Veiled Realm's power?"

The figure paused. "Our king waits. But not idly. He has not forgotten betrayal."

A sharp rumble echoed beneath their feet.

Eris turned toward the hall entrance. "Something's moving out there."

The lights above flickered violently. The masked figure raised a hand.

"You have opened the path, Evelyn. Now you must walk it. Go—before the Veil sees you as an intruder."

A hidden door cracked open behind them, leading to a winding path of obsidian stairs climbing back toward the forest above.

"But wait," Evelyn said, "Who are you?"

The figure stepped back into the dark.

"A reminder," they whispered. "That silence is never empty."

And then they were gone.

The ground shuddered again—deeper this time, angrier.

Joren grabbed Evelyn's arm. "We have to move. Now."

They ran—through the sacred hall, up the spiraling stair, the glowing orbs blinking out behind them one by one. The forest met them with a cold wind as they burst back into the clearing, the stone monolith now shattered at its center.

And behind them, the stairway sealed shut—roots knitting together, stone groaning as it folded inward, hiding the path they had taken. It was as though the Veil itself had closed its eye.

Evelyn fell to her knees, breathing hard, palms glowing like coals. Her mind burned with everything she had learned. The betrayal. The manipulation. The lie of protection.

The truth had been buried deep.

And she had just uncovered it.

CHAPTER NINETEEN

THE SILENT WAR

The forest no longer felt still.

It had only been a few days since Evelyn and her friends made their way back from the hidden shrine, but already, the atmosphere in Brantham was changing. It wasn't anything dramatic or earth-shattering, but rather a series of subtle hints—like the wisps of mist that danced through the outer woods, unexpected chills that swept in out of nowhere, and trees that creaked as if they were alive, even in the stillness. The Veil had been disturbed, and something old and powerful was stirring within it.

Evelyn found herself at the edge of the woods, the very spot where they had first stepped out. Her eyes were lost in thought, staring into the distance. The stone monolith was completely gone—there was no sign of the entrance left, just a circle of darker soil where the roots had woven the earth back together.

Behind her, Joren approached. "Another one was found this morning."

She turned to him, brows furrowed. "Another what?"

"A patch of Veil-mist hung over the northern fields. Eris attempted to clear it away, but it just wouldn't budge. The farmers are feeling a bit on edge."

Evelyn nodded grimly. This wasn't just residual energy—they were being watched.

Inside the village council hall—now a cozy hub for Evelyn's strategic planning—she gathered with Eris and Joren. Meanwhile, Siora stayed back, skillfully overseeing the gentle shifts in the land and looking after the villagers, who were starting to feel that something much bigger was brewing just beneath the surface.

"There's definitely a pattern to these appearances," Eris remarked, pointing at a chart he had drawn. "They seem to trace the ley—oh, I mean the ancient conduits—of energy that connect the realms. It's as if something is testing the limits."

"Or someone," Evelyn muttered.

Joren crossed his arms. "You think the Veiled King knows what we saw?"

Eris shrugged, but his face was serious. "We trespassed in his forgotten temple. The Veil isn't just a place—it's alive. It listens."

That night, sleep did not come easy.

Evelyn envisioned a throne crafted from roots and stone, enveloped in a veil of smoke. rested upon it was a figure draped in shadows, his face hidden by a mask adorned with black antlers. His voice resonated through the darkness:

"You defy what was sealed. You tear open what was meant to remain shut."

When Evelyn woke, her hands were glowing faintly, and the moon outside had turned crimson. Eris rushed to her door moments later—he had seen the same vision. Joren stood at the edge of the village, sword drawn.

"Something came through," he said.

They found it near the southern edge—a being that seemed almost otherworldly. Mist wrapped around its form, which was vaguely human in shape, adorned with bone-like spikes and eyes that shone a bright blue. It was silent as it stepped out from between the trees, but the pressure in the air grew thick and suffocating. It radiated Veil energy—cold and ancient.

Without warning, the creature attacked.

Joren faced the creature bravely, his sword meeting its razor-sharp claws with a loud clash. The steel barely made a dent. Meanwhile, Evelyn's markings started to glow, and as she approached, the creature hesitated, pulling back from her aura. She reached out her hand, and in response to her silent command, the light from her markings burst forth, hitting the beast like a powerful spear.

It staggered, letting out a shriek that felt like it was scraping against bone. Eris began to chant a binding incantation, weaving symbols in the air that wrapped around the creature like glowing chains. But it wasn't going down without a fight—tendrils of mist lashed out, knocking Eris to the ground.

Joren delivered a powerful strike, slicing through a portion of the creature's misty limb. Meanwhile, Evelyn stood her ground, focusing intently. Her markings flared up with a fierce glow, and this time, the light enveloped the creature entirely.

With a howl that echoed through the trees, it fell apart into a mist, blending back into the ground. The only trace left behind was a lone symbol etched into the earth: a spiral with wings on either side.

Eris crouched beside it. "It's a message."

"From him," Evelyn whispered. "He's watching."

In the days after the attack, Evelyn's determination grew stronger. She realized that just having power wasn't sufficient—neither raw instinct nor fear-driven reflexes would cut it. What she needed was precision, control, and discipline. And so, her training began.

Every morning, Evelyn would meet Joren in the glade just outside Brantham, where the fog still hung in the air, but the sunlight peeked through in beautiful golden strands. In this serene spot, surrounded by tall grass and ancient trees, he put her through her paces in swordplay. At first, she was a bit too reactive, hesitant and relying too much on instinct. But Joren, with his endless patience and practical approach, guided her to pause, to observe her opponent's body language before they made a move, and to transform her defense into offense. He never went easy on her; every bruise and every tumble was hard-earned. "Your enemy won't show you any mercy," he reminded her. "And neither will the Veil."

Afternoons were a special time spent with Eris, diving deep into study and finding spiritual harmony. He led her through ancient rituals, spoken in a language older than the realms, and taught her breathing techniques that connected her spirit to the powerful forces awakening inside her. They would meditate by the old stone circle, where the markings on Evelyn's hands would come alive—glowing softly whenever she became still enough to listen to their gentle hum. With Eris's guidance, she discovered how to channel their light without exhausting herself. It wasn't just about magic; it was about tapping into the memories woven into her very bloodline, responding to her call.

Some evenings, she found herself training alone—gracefully flowing through sword forms atop the hill, her blade cutting through the mist and moonlight. She would whisper her questions to the stars, though they offered no replies: Who had placed this power in her? Why her? And would she be strong enough when the time came?

The villagers watched from a respectful distance, some awed, others fearful. But slowly, as her control improved, so did their trust.

One night, as she stood overlooking the forest below, markings gently pulsing in time with her breath, Evelyn realized she no longer feared the power within her.

She was becoming something else—something forged.

Something ready.

One afternoon, a raven landed on her windowsill. Its eyes glinted in a strange way. Clutched in its claw was a scroll, sealed with bright red wax. Evelyn picked it up gently, intrigued by the mysterious delivery.

The message inside was written in ink that shimmered with silver:

You are not the first flame. But you may be the last. Cross again, and the fire will come for you.

There was no signature.

"He's threatened me before," Evelyn said, burning the letter. "But now he's afraid. He knows I'm real."

By the sixth day, whispers had reached the other realms. Allies sent coded messages—some in support of her vision of unity. Others warned her to stop. But Evelyn had made up her mind.

As twilight fell on the seventh day, she climbed the hill overlooking Brantham. Eris and Joren joined her, silent but steady.

Far in the distance, beyond the mists, the skies over the Veiled Realm began to glow with unnatural light—green and silver threads dancing in the heavens.

Then the sky shifted—not visibly, not yet, but sensed. A thunderless sound echoed through the land. A storm without wind.

And a voice.

"The chosen flame has been kindled."

Evelyn fell to one knee, clutching her chest as the markings blazed across her skin.

"Now let her burn."

The markings on Evelyn's skin burst into light, spiraling with radiant power as the wind howled around them. The trees bent back. The sky shimmered.

And just behind them, the earth began to shift ever so slightly. Vines moved gracefully, resembling lazy rivers, as the soil nestled back into its rightful spot. Roots extended like fingers across the gap, and then, with a gentle quiver, the forest floor was complete again.

No scar. No crack. No opening.

Only silence, and the subtle breath of the trees.

It was not a door slamming shut—it was something older, quieter. A ritual sealed. A trial passed, or perhaps merely begun.

Evelyn stood slowly, her legs unsteady, her gaze fixed on the closed earth. Whatever lay ahead, they could not go back the way they came. The realms had shifted. The game had changed.

And the Veil would not rest.

CHAPTER TWENTY

SHADOWS AT THE GATE

The once solid unity of Evelyn's inner circle was beginning to crack.

Inside the revamped council hall in Brantham—where the stone walls are now adorned with maps, letters, and artifacts—the atmosphere was charged with tension. The long oak table, which used to be a spot for shared visions and calm strategies, had transformed into a battleground of hidden disputes and unvoiced anxieties.

Joren stood with his arms crossed near the hearth, brow furrowed. "We're not ready for open conflict. The people aren't soldiers. You saw how they looked at you last night—half of them afraid, the rest unsure."

Eris leaned forward, voice low but firm. "Fear doesn't mean doubt. They follow her because she gives them hope. That light? That was no accident. It was a sign."

"And signs don't stop swords," Joren shot back.

Evelyn remained at the head of the table, her hands resting on the surface, fingers gently tapping in a slow rhythm. She hadn't spoken yet, letting the tide of the argument wash around her.

Thessa, one of the village's elder healers and a recent member of the council, finally spoke up, breaking the silence. "We need to look beyond our own concerns. The Veiled Realm is awakening. Evelyn, your markings—they've disrupted the balance. There are ancient forces at work here, far beyond what we fear."

"But people are frightened," said Bram, a young scout. "Last night, three families left. Packed up before dawn. Said they didn't want to be caught between realms."

Evelyn finally rose to her feet, her demeanor serene yet powerful. "And where do you think they would go?" Her tone was steady, but her words sliced through the mounting anxiety. "No realm is free from danger. Do you really believe that silence or giving up will protect them?"

The room stilled. No one had an answer.

She looked to each of them in turn. "I did not ask to be marked. I did not ask to be chosen. But the Veil is moving, and so must we. If the realms remain fractured, we fall alone. If we unite them, we stand a chance."

Joren exhaled heavily and looked away.

Eris finally nodded. "Then we need to prepare. Not just for battle—but for diplomacy. For truth. For a future."

As the evening settled in, the room gradually cleared out, leaving Evelyn by herself. The warm glow of the firelight created playful shadows that danced along the walls, and her eyes were drawn to the old map hanging next to the window—not a map of places, but a tapestry of tales: kingdoms, secrets, and betrayals.

They were no longer just her enemies.

They were her inheritance.

And something in the dark was watching how she would wield it.

A heavy knock broke the quiet.

Evelyn glanced away from the dancing flames of the hearth just as the door let out a soft creak. Bram burst in, panting and covered in mud, gripping the doorframe for support

"There's someone—at the edge of the village," he gasped. "Says he's from the Veiled Realm. He's not... attacking. He's asking to speak with you, Evelyn."

Joren reappeared behind Bram, weapon already at his hip. "It could be a trap."

"Or a message," Thessa murmured from behind, drawn by the commotion.

Evelyn's thoughts were in a whirlwind. The Veiled Realm had never sent messengers unless they had a specific agenda. She gave a quick nod. "Let him in. But make sure he's unarmed."

Minutes later, the village hall fell into a tense silence as the doors opened again, revealing the figure standing in the threshold.

He stood tall, wrapped in a deep gray cloak that seemed to shimmer like mist when the torchlight hit it. A thin veil of fabric partially obscured his face, but his eyes sparkled with an unusual light. Instead of stepping forward right away, he bowed— not a deep bow, but one done with careful intention.

"I come on behalf of the Veiled King," he said, his voice smooth, almost too controlled. "I am called Maerel. And I bring a warning."

Eris leaned in closer to Evelyn, lowering her voice. "He's not just any representative. That shimmer... it's ancient magic."

Maerel kept his eyes locked on Evelyn as he spoke. "You've awakened powers that were supposed to remain asleep. Those markings on your hands? They're not a gift, at least not for us—they're a danger. The Veiled Realm doesn't want conflict, but it won't submit to chaos."

Evelyn rose from her chair, stepping forward with calm authority. "Then why come here? Why now?"

"Listen," Maerel said firmly, "our King wants you to be clear on this: if you take even one more step toward entering our territory, he'll see it as a declaration of war. No more games. No more hints. Just pure fire."

Evelyn clenched her jaw, her voice steady but filled with intensity. "And what about the fires he's started in the past? The broken realms? The barrier he created to separate us?"

Maerel stayed silent. Yet, in the stillness that hung in the air, the flames in the hearth flickered oddly, creating elongated, peculiar shadows that danced around the room.

He bowed once more. "The decision lies with you, Princess. Or... perhaps no longer a Princess."

Then he turned and walked out into the night without another word.

Eris broke the silence. "That was no envoy. That was a challenge."

Thessa nodded grimly. "And he knew exactly what he was doing. Fear divides faster than swords."

As the envoy disappeared into the swirling mists outside, a wave of murmurs swept through the villagers who had gathered nearby. Whispers flitted from one person to another—some filled with fear, others bubbling with anger. A woman tightened her grip on her child, while a group of farmers cast wary glances at the council hall, their suspicion noticeable.

"That creature didn't belong here," someone muttered. "They've brought danger to our gates."

"They'll bring war if she keeps going," another hissed.

The voices began to rise, weaving a bitter tension through Brantham's peaceful night. Some villagers stood their ground, their eyes filled with a cautious resolve, while others appeared ready to flee—or even worse, to fight back.

Evelyn stared into the fire, her mind already moving faster than her words could catch up. The council was breaking. Her enemies were circling. And now, the Veiled Realm had made its first move across the board.

But she wasn't about to back down.

"We hold a council at dawn," she said. "The Veiled King wants war? Let's decide how we'll answer."

Outside, the wind howled through Brantham's streets, and somewhere beyond, the mist of the Veil thickened—as if listening.

CHAPTER TWENTY-ONE

THE WAITING STORM

The cold wind rolled through Brantham like a silent warning.

As the first light of dawn crept in, the village was enveloped in a thick mist, revealing a scene unlike anything it had ever witnessed before. The council hall, which used to be a simple wooden and stone structure, had undergone a remarkable transformation. The walls were adorned with charts detailing weather patterns, diagrams of ley-channels, and strategic sketches. In the center stood a war table, hewn from a fallen oak tree, its surface marked with rough maps of the realms—routes that were once thought to be sealed off, and landscapes both familiar and shrouded in mystery.

Evelyn stood at its center, her hand hovering over a thin line drawn from Brantham to the ancient Hollow Crossings—one of the few weak points where the veil between realms thinned. Her markings glowed faintly, a soft rhythm pulsing with her thoughts.

Around her, the room stirred.

Joren paced, arms behind his back. "We've moved the scouts to the northern ridges. Eris and I believe they're close. There's been movement. Fires seen in the trees."

"They're watching us," Eris added from near the doorway. "The Veiled King won't wait forever. He wanted a war. He'll have it soon."

Siora leaned forward, fingers steepled. "Not just any war. He's forcing a confrontation on his terms, not ours. If you strike first, Evelyn, you play into his hands. But wait too long... and he'll crush the people's resolve before a sword is ever drawn."

Evelyn looked down at the map. Her jaw tightened. "Then we don't strike first. We strike... wisely."

Outside, Brantham had fallen silent. The usual hustle and bustle of preparations had quieted down under Evelyn's new command: there would be no grand assembly, no armies gearing up for battle. This wasn't a fight meant for the villagers.

This was hers alone.

The people still watched, still waited—but not for orders. For outcome.

Evelyn strolled through the village, her hood pulled down to shield her face. As she walked, she noticed families gathered around flickering fires, elders carefully weaving protective charms into the edges of their cloaks, and quiet figures placing candles on windowsills, casting a warm glow in the dim evening.

Each face she passed felt etched into her bones.

When she returned to the council chamber, Thessa stood waiting with an ancient scroll held in trembling hands.

"This was buried beneath the shrine," she said. "I never understood what it meant until now."

Evelyn carefully unrolled the brittle parchment, the ink still vibrant and bold. It revealed an ancient prophecy, swirling in intricate spirals and circles, depicting the coming together of three realms through a chosen soul—not one destined to rule, but to mend and reshape what had been shattered.

"She's not just a leader," Thessa whispered. "She's the balance."

That evening, Evelyn gathered her council, her most trusted allies, and the village's wisest storytellers around the warm glow of the fire outside the hall. She didn't wear a crown or any armor—just her markings, which shimmered on her skin like a radiant light.

"I won't offer false hope," she began. "What's coming may break us. It may bury everything we've built. But I will not run from it. Not for a throne. Not for legacy. I was born in silence, but I choose to speak now."

Eyes locked on her, every breath held.

"The Veiled King didn't rule through cruelty; he ruled with authority. He brought the realms under his control with a mix of strength and foresight, casting a long shadow over them. He didn't destroy them, but he also never allowed them to flourish. By making unity unattainable, he ensured that his power remained unchallenged."

A ripple of unease stirred the circle.

"I will not answer dominance with war. I will not restore balance with the same tools that broke it. But I will face him—and I will end this divide. One way or another."

She raised her hand, palm open. "At dawn, I go alone. This fight was never meant for all of you. It began with me. And it will end with me."

Joren stepped forward, voice low. "You'll need someone at your back. I'm coming."

Evelyn shook her head gently. "If I fall, someone must remain to protect what we've begun here. That's you."

Then Eris stepped forward, defiance flickering in his eyes. "You're not going alone. I've followed you through storms and shadows, and I'm not stopping now."

"Eris—"

"No." He cut in firmly. "You said this ends with you. But maybe... it's supposed to begin with both of us. Let me stand with you."

Evelyn hesitated, eyes searching his. Then she gave a small nod. "All right. We go together."

The circle quieted again, reverent.

And behind her, from the forest's edge, a glow shimmered faintly in the trees—watching, waiting.

The storm hadn't broken yet.

But the wind had changed direction.

CHAPTER TWENTY-TWO

THE UNVEILING

The forest had changed.

Evelyn sensed it in the way the wind didn't merely blow but seemed to whisper, as if the trees were in on some secret about what was ahead. Roots twisted with purpose, and shadows huddled closer between the trunks. The Veiled Realm felt vibrant, conscious, and ever-watchful.

Eris walked beside her, his steps quieter than usual. He hadn't said much since they left the glade, not out of fear but focus. His hand rested on the hilt of his blade, and his eyes scanned every flicker of movement. They had passed the point of no return an hour ago, and still the trail pulled them deeper, tighter, toward the heart.

Toward the King.

Evelyn came to a stop at a rise in the path, where the mist cleared just enough for her to catch a glimpse of the horizon. In the distance, towering peaks stood tall, their snowy tops cutting through the violet sky. But what truly took her breath away was the sight right in front of her—a colossal spire of black stone jutting up from the forest floor like a shard of night. It seemed to pulse with a soft red glow, almost as if it were breathing.

"That's it," she said. "The Hollow Spire."

Eris nodded grimly. "And he's waiting inside."

They descended in silence. No birdsong accompanied them. No wind stirred the trees. The silence thickened the closer they came, a silence that weighed on Evelyn's shoulders like armor. Her markings burned faintly beneath her gloves.

The gates of the Hollow Spire stood open.

The moment they stepped into the entry hall, warmth closed around them like a cloak. Not comfort—no, this heat was sharp and unnatural. The walls inside the Spire shimmered like obsidian, etched with symbols Evelyn couldn't read. Light glowed from within the walls, as though the stone had swallowed stars.

And at the far end of the hall, upon a throne carved from the same black stone, sat the King of the Veiled Realm.

He rose slowly.

He was not cloaked in darkness, as Evelyn had imagined. No, he wore robes of deep crimson and silver, embroidered with constellations. His hair fell long and white over his shoulders, and his eyes—those eyes burned like suns behind storm clouds.

"You came," he said, voice resonant and smooth. "Just as it was written."

Evelyn stepped forward. "I came for answers. For truth."

The King smiled, and it was not cruel. "You came to end what your father began."

Eris drew his blade. Evelyn raised a hand to stop him. "Not yet."

The King stepped down from the dais, each step echoing through the chamber. "Aldric feared me," he said. "He feared what I represented. Not destruction. Balance. Unity. Power not controlled by crowns, but by purpose."

"Then why did you cut off the realms?" Evelyn pressed. "What's the reason for shutting this world away behind the Veil?"

"Because your father made unity impossible. He stole from us, twisted prophecy, and turned allies into enemies. When the other kings turned their backs, I did the only thing I could. I protected what remained."

Eris scoffed. "You dominated the others. You let the Veil become a wound that never healed."

The King turned his gaze to Eris. "Because the wound was never allowed to."

Evelyn felt her blood rise, the markings on her skin flaring to life. "And now it's time to mend it."

"You would undo what kept us alive?"

"I would free what was imprisoned. I would rebuild what was broken."

The King's expression darkened. "Then you choose war."

A powerful gust swept through the hall as he lifted his hand. The symbols adorning the walls erupted in a brilliant glow. Evelyn was knocked backward, sliding across the smooth floor. Eris rushed ahead, his blade gleaming. The King countered with a spear of light he conjured.

The battle ignited.

Eris faced off against the King, their weapons clashing loudly in the chamber. Evelyn struggled to her feet, pain radiating from her side, and released a powerful burst of energy from her hands. Her markings glowed a brilliant gold, transforming into whips of light that coiled around the King's arm. He let out a snarl and broke free, tossing Eris aside with a swift motion.

"You think you understand power," the King said, summoning a storm of blades from the air. "You are a child of stolen stories!"

Evelyn summoned a radiant shield, and the blades shattered upon impact. With determination, she surged forward, her hand igniting into a sword of brilliant flames. When it clashed with the King's spear, the collision erupted in a shower of sparks that danced across the stone.

"I'm the flame you tried to bury!"

They clashed fiercely in the hallway, magic crackling all around them. Pillars splintered, and the floor buckled beneath their feet. Eris found his balance again and launched a flurry of well-aimed strikes to keep the King occupied. Meanwhile, Evelyn darted in from the side, her blade just barely brushing against his shoulder. The King let out a furious roar and unleashed a wave of energy, sending both of them crashing to the ground.

He towered over Evelyn, spear held high. "You would ruin everything I've fought to protect."

"No," she gasped, markings flaring, eyes glowing. "I will restore it."

Evelyn shot her hands up into the air. Suddenly, the floor below them cracked open, and a burst of light exploded from the fissure. The King lost his balance and stumbled. With a surge of energy coursing through her, Evelyn stood tall and charged ahead, plunging her blade deep into the obsidian at his feet.

A shockwave tore through the chamber. The walls pulsed. The symbols dimmed.

The King fell to one knee.

Evelyn stood over him, chest heaving. "It ends now."

The King looked up, blood at the corner of his mouth. He smiled, faintly. "Then let it end. But know this: unity is not peace. It is conflict made honest."

Evelyn lowered her hand. "I'll take that over lies."

The King collapsed, unconscious.

Silence returned.

Eris limped to her side. "Is it over?"

Evelyn looked around the shattered hall. The markings on her skin faded to a faint glow. Outside, the forest began to breathe again.

"No," she said softly. "But it's beginning."

And far above, unseen, the Veil rippled—thin, trembling.

About to break.

CHAPTER TWENTY-THREE

THE QUIET END

The journey home was quieter than Evelyn had imagined.

The Veil had been lifted. The balance between realms had changed, and the Hollow Spire stood quiet in the center of the forest. But the world didn't rejoice or burst into celebration. Instead, it let out a gentle sigh. Softly. Slowly. As if it were rediscovering how to breathe once more.

Evelyn leaned against the balcony railing of the council chamber, her eyes wandering over the stone courtyards of the capital. The banners that once fluttered proudly had been removed, and the crown she had once been destined to wear still hadn't found its way back to its rightful place.

It was no longer her weight to carry.

Yet, one final spark still flickered in the remnants of her past.

King Aldric.

He hadn't been seen since before the battle, and rumors were running wild. Some said he had escaped to the northern bays, while others hinted at his exile to a coastal hideaway once favored by ancestors in search of peace. It was to this very place that Evelyn now rode, the wind gently tugging at her cloak, her markings faint yet unwavering on her skin.

She found him in a garden of frost-touched herbs, overlooking the sea.

He did not rise when she approached.

"You came," he said quietly, without turning.

"You knew I would."

Aldric finally turned to her. His once mighty figure appeared diminished, not just by the passage of time, but by something more profound, maybe it was regret, or the heavy burden of finally being truly seen.

"You won," he said. "The realms are mending. The Veil is no longer sealed. You ended what I began."

Evelyn's voice was steel wrapped in silk. "What you began was a lie. You stole unity and called it safety. You silenced truths and named it peace."

"I did what I had to," Aldric said, but his words lacked conviction. They felt more like the echoes of a man desperately trying to rationalize a past filled with dominance.

"No," she replied, taking a step closer. "You did what you wanted to. You were scared of losing control over everything, and when you felt that power was at risk from the Veil King, from the prophecy, from me—you decided to turn your back on it all."

His eyes flinched, just slightly.

"You locked away the truth. You turned realms into rivals. You tried to mold me into something I'm not. And when I began to see through you, you vanished."

Aldric sat down heavily on the stone bench behind him. "Would you have preferred me dead on that throne?"

"No," Evelyn said. "I wanted you to confront your actions. As a king should. As a father should."

He gazed at her in that moment, really taking her in. And whatever he had planned to say just faded away, stuck on his lips.

Evelyn allowed the silence to linger, the sound of the ocean crashing against the cliffs echoing in the background. "I'm not seeking revenge," she finally broke the quiet. "You don't deserve that. But I needed you to hear this. To understand that your rule didn't come to an end with a battle, but with the truth finally being voiced."

She turned, cloak catching the wind. Aldric did not call after her.

As she mounted her horse and rode back toward the capital, Evelyn felt something loosen within her.

Not forgiveness.

But freedom.

And when she reached the gates, the sun was rising over the distant trees, and the road ahead was wide, unruled, and finally her own.

Villagers, once divided and wary, now looked to Evelyn—not as a ruler, but as a symbol.

She walked among them without guards, no longer burdened by ceremony or crown. Where once they bowed, now they nodded with quiet respect. Children chased each other through the square with ribbons the color of dawn. A smith, scarred from past battles, offered her a cup of water and a tired smile. There was no pageantry in their trust—only something slow, healing, and real.

Still, Evelyn felt the pull of silence.

That evening, she quietly left the capital and made her way along a well-known path to the hill just past the old orchard. There, nestled among the grasses swaying in the breeze, stood a small memorial. The stone didn't have a title or any royal symbol, just her mother's name, lovingly carved in soft, flowing letters.

Evelyn knelt beside it.

The wind gently rustled the wildflowers at its feet. She embraced the quiet, reminiscing about the times her mother would braid her hair, the sound of her laughter echoing through sunlit hallways before the weight of politics dulled all that was bright.

"I did it, Mother," she said softly. "Not as they wanted me to. Not as they planned. But I did it. And I'm still here."

She traced the carvings with her fingertips. "I lost so much. And I learned more than I ever wanted to. About them. About myself."

A pause.

"I think you always knew."

Above her, the sky transformed into a canvas of stars. She didn't shed a tear. Not this time. Instead, she took a moment to breathe. One slow inhale. One steady exhale.

A life had ended. A war had closed.

But Evelyn's story wasn't done yet.

She rose, the markings on her skin now dim as embers—but still there. Still burning with quiet purpose.

And as she turned back toward the road that led home, the first fireflies of spring lit the path before her.

Epilogue

The wind carried the scent of wet earth and wildflowers through the glade. Trees that had once stood as silent witnesses to battle now bent gently in the breeze, their branches full of life, their roots untouched by war. The land was healing.

So was she.

Evelyn found herself standing at the edge of the lake—the very same one where, ages ago, she had woken up feeling disoriented and unsure. The water mirrored the pristine sky above, calm and untouched. As she gazed into the lake, her reflection danced with the gentle ripples, revealing the faint shimmer of the symbols still imprinted on her skin. They didn't sting or throb anymore; instead, they pulsed softly, like a steady heartbeat—there, but no longer insistent.

Behind her, voices rose in the distance: laughter, conversation, the soft rhythm of life returning. The three realms, once torn by secrets and silence, were no longer fractured. Not united fully, not yet—but speaking, trading, remembering. A council of new leaders had emerged, drawn from all corners. Evelyn had helped build it, but she no longer sat among them.

She had abdicated her claim to the crown, and with it, the expectations that once defined her. Now, her path was her own.

A rustle behind her.

"You always seem to seek out the quietest spots," Eris remarked as he appeared. His cloak was speckled with pollen and bits of leaves. He had a satchel slung over his shoulder, filled with letters and books—news from beyond the mountains, along with his ever-expanding collection of peculiar stories and even stranger truths.

Evelyn smiled. "Some things don't change."

He joined her by the water's edge. They stood without speaking for a while, letting the silence stretch.

"The border towns are holding well," Eris said eventually. "Trade is steady. And Joren says the southern coast finally elected a council without shouting matches. Progress."

"And the Veil Realm?"

Eris nodded. "Opening, slowly. Still wary. But they've started sharing their healing knowledge. I think they want to believe this peace will last."

Evelyn watched a dragonfly skim the water's surface. "They deserve peace. We all do."

He glanced at her, curious. "Do you ever think of it—what it could've been like, if the prophecy had never come to pass?"

She gazed up at the sky. The sun peeked through the passing clouds, casting a warm, golden glow

"Sometimes. But then I remember... this. The stillness. The chance to choose. And I wouldn't trade it."

Eris chuckled. "You know, there are whispers you might return one day. That the Chosen One has simply gone to sleep for a while."

Evelyn shook her head with a grin. "Let them whisper. I'm done being a symbol. I want to be someone who plants things—and watches them grow."

Further down the path, a child's laughter rang out. Evelyn turned to see villagers setting up for the spring celebration. Lanterns swung from trees. Baskets overflowed with bread and early berries.

Her gaze softened. This, too, was power. Quiet. Patient. Rooted in trust.

She dug into her satchel and fished out a tattered letter—its edges crinkled and the ink softened by the years. Aldric's handwriting still lingered on the page, a ghost of memories. She didn't read it anymore, but it stayed with her, a reminder of things that should never fade from memory.

Betrayal did not define her.

Nor did destiny.

She carefully folded the letter again and set it down next to a stone at the edge of the lake, allowing the wind to gently lift her fingers as if saying goodbye.

The realms were watching, yes. But not for prophecy or power.

They were watching a new world unfold.

And Evelyn, no longer heir, no longer chosen—was simply part of it.

A woman with a voice, a past, and a future still her own.

www.ingramcontent.com/pod-product-compliance
Lightning Source LLC
Chambersburg PA
CBHW020611160726
47991CB00002BA/724